A Kind of Spark

Elle McNicoll

Published by Knights Of
Knights Of Ltd, Registered Offices: 119 Marylebone Road, London, NW1 5PU

www.knightsof.media
First published 2020
002

Written by Elle McNicoll
Text and cover copyright © Elle McNicoll, 2020
Cover art by © Kay Wilson, 2020

Set in Baskerville Regular / 12 pt
Typeset design by Marssaié Jordan
Printed and bound in the UK

A CIP catalogue record for this book will be available from the British Library

ISBN: 9781913311056

2 4 6 8 10 9 7 5 3

A Kind of Spark

of

Spark

ELLE McNICOLL

For Mum, Dad and Josh.
And all children with happy, flapping hands.

Chapter One

"This handwriting is utterly disgraceful."

I hear the words but they seem far away. As if they are being shouted through a wall. I continue to stare at the piece of paper in front of me. I can read it. I can make out every word, even through the blurriness of tears. I can feel everyone in the classroom watching me. My best friend. Her new friend. The new girl. Some of the boys are laughing.

I just keep staring at my writing. Then, suddenly, it's gone.

Miss Murphy has snatched it from my desk and is now ripping it up. The sound of the paper being torn is overly loud. Right in my ears. The characters in the story I was writing beg her to stop, but she doesn't. She crumples it all together and throws it towards the classroom bin. She misses. My story lies in a heap on the scratchy carpet.

"Do not EVER write so lazily again," she shouts. Maybe she isn't even shouting, but it feels that way. "Do you hear me, Adeline?" I prefer being called Addie. "Not ever. A girl your age knows better than to write like that; your handwriting is like a baby's."

I wish my sister was here. Keedie always explains the things that I cannot control or explain for myself. She makes sense of them. She understands.

"Tell me that you understand?"

Her shouts are so loud and the moments after are so quiet. I nod, shakily. Even though I don't understand. I just know it's what I'm supposed to do.

She says nothing more. She moves to the front of the class and I am dismissed. I can feel the new girl glancing at me, and my friend Jenna is whispering to her new friend, Emily.

We were supposed to have Mrs Bright this year; we met her briefly before the summer holidays. She would draw a little sun with a smiling face beside her name and would hold your hand if you looked nervous. But she got sick and Miss Murphy came to teach our class instead.

I thought this new school year would be better. That I would be better.

I take out my pocket thesaurus. It was a Christmas present from Keedie. She knows how much I love using different words and we laughed because the word 'thesaurus' sounds like a dinosaur. I read different word combinations to calm down, to process the shouting and the ripping.

I find one that I like. Diminished.

On days like this, I spend lunchtime in the library. I feel the other children in the class watching me as we tuck in our chairs and leave the room, the school bell screeching so loudly. Loud noises make my head spin, they feel like a drill against a sensitive nerve. I walk through the corridors, practicing my breathing and keeping my eyes straight ahead. People talk so loudly to their friends, who are right next to them. They get too close, they push and clamour, and it makes my neck hot and my heart too quick.

But, when I finally get to the library, it's all quiet. There is so much space. There is one window open to let in a little fresh air. There is no loud talking allowed. The books are all categorised and labelled in their proper places.

And Mr Allison is at his desk.

"Addie!"

He has curly dark hair and big glasses, and he is tall and skinny for a man. He wears old jumpers. If I were to use my thesaurus to describe Mr Allison, I would say he was kindly.

But I like to just say that he is nice. Because he is. My brain is very visual. I see everything in specific pictures, and when people use the word "nice", I think of Mr Allison, the librarian.

"I have just the thing for you!"

I like that he never asks boring questions. He doesn't ask how my holidays were or how my sisters are doing. He just gets straight to talking about books.

"Here we go." He walks over to one of the reading tables and puts a large hardback book down in front of me. I feel all the horrid feelings from earlier disappear.

"Sharks!"

I flip it open immediately and stroke the first glossy page. I told Mr Allison last year that I love sharks. That they are the most interesting thing to me, even more than the ancient Egyptians and the dinosaurs.

He remembered.

"It's a sort of encyclopedia," he tells me, as I sit down with the book. "An encyclopedia is a book that tells you a lot about one subject, or one area of study. This one is all about sharks."

I nod, somewhat dazed from excitement.

"I suspect you know everything that's in there already though," he says, and he laughs after he says it so I know that he's joking.

"Sharks don't have bones," I tell him, caressing the photograph of what I know is a blue shark. "And they have six senses. Not five. They can sort of sense electricity in the atmosphere. The electricity of life!

They can also smell blood from miles away."

Their senses are sometimes overpowering. Too loud, too strong, too much of everything.

I turn the page to a large photograph of a solitary Greenland shark, swimming alone in the ice-cold water.

"People don't understand them." I touch the shark's fin. "They hate them, actually. A lot of people. They're afraid of them and don't understand them. So, they try to hurt them."

Mr Allison doesn't say anything for a while, as I read the first page.

"You take that home with you for as long as you would like, Addie."

I look up at him. He is smiling, but his eyes don't match his mouth.

"Thank you!" I make sure to put all the glad that I am feeling into my voice so that he knows I really mean it. He moves back to his desk and I become engrossed in the book. Reading is the most calming thing after an overly loud and unkind classroom. I can take my time. There is no one rushing me or barking at me. The words all follow rules. The pictures are bright and alive. But they do not overpower me.

When I am trying to sleep at night, I like to imagine diving beneath the cold waves of the ocean and swimming with a shark. We explore abandoned shipwrecks, underwater caves and coral reefs. All of the colour, but in a wide-open space. No crowds, no pushing and no taking. I would not grab their dorsal fin. We would swim alongside one another.

And we would not have to speak a word. We could just be.

Chapter Two

Waiting for my sister is the longest time of the day.

Dad is already cooking by the time I arrive home from school. Today is Monday, so dinner will be pasta. I like it quite plain. Too much sauce makes my tongue feel like it's drowning so Dad makes a white sauce for me, and a different one for the rest of the family: Dad, and my two older sisters, and Mum when she's not at work.

"Tea's almost ready, Addie."

Dad knows not to ask me questions straight away. I need time to settle. That's what Keedie says, she's the one who told me that and then she told Dad. Since then, it's been easier.

I help set the table and we throw pasta onto the ceiling to see if it will stick. One piece falls down and Dad catches it in his mouth. He laughs and eats it before yelling upstairs for Nina to finish talking to her camera and come down for dinner. He cannot hear the scrape of her chair, the whirring of her camera lens as it retracts, or the resigned click of her bedroom door closing.

But I can.

Nina is my other older sister, always here and always wanting. What she wants, I'm not really sure. A different house, a more perfect life. The kind of life she pretends to live in her videos. A rose gold life that's neat and tidy.

She has auburn hair that she dyes blonde and only sensible piercings. She wears tartan skirts and turtle necks. Her bedroom has a camera on a tall tripod and important looking lights. She talks to tens of thousands of people through her camera, about clothes and make-up.

She smiles on her videos in a way I have never seen her smile off camera.

"What's today's video about?"

Dad asks regular and repetitive questions. He calls it "making an effort". He says it's important for letting people know that you're interested in their lives. If I'm interested in someone, I have hundreds of questions for them, and they are never the same.

"Just a Q&A," Nina replies, spooning a small portion of pasta onto her plate. The smell of the sauce that she drizzles over the dish stings my nostrils. "My views have dipped since I stopped doing hauls."

Mum told her that buying large amounts of clothes each month was wasteful. It was a big argument. Doors were slammed and it made my hands tremble.

Nina gets up and goes to the fridge, wrenching it open to grab a bottle of juice. "Where is she?"

I've realised that Nina speaks with a certain tone of voice when she's talking about Keedie. Her voice is visual, two different colours. One is dark and one is light. Both colours are for Keedie. But I'm not sure what they mean.

Nina is not the sister I'm waiting for. Keedie is.

Dad does not answer her, and I know she wasn't talking to me, because she wasn't looking at me. I wrap a piece of pasta around my fork. It takes a while.

"How was school?" I can feel Nina's eyes staring right at my shoulders. So, I shrug them. She moves to sit with us at the table. "I asked you a question, Addie."

"Nina."

Dad rebukes her gently.

"Don't remember." It isn't a lie, like Nina goes on to accuse. It all becomes difficult to piece together once I'm out of the school building. It will fall into place as a memory over the next couple of days.

"You have an excellent memory," Nina tells me, scraping her cutlery against her plate in a way that makes me feel ill. "If she's telling us she can't remember, something must be wrong."

She's talking to Dad now.

"Do you like your teacher?"

Images of Miss Murphy flash behind my eyes. Her one really yellow tooth. Her long fingernails. "She's just like Keedie said."

Nina brings her cutlery down sharply. "You see… you're just basing your opinion on what Keedie told you. She taught Keedie a long time ago, Addie. It's been just over one week, you can't know what she's like."

"Then why did you ask me?"

I don't understand Nina. She wants things out of our conversations that I don't know how to give. She talks to the people who watch her videos like she loves them. I watch her sometimes. When I was doing my Saturday therapy, the man would place photographs in front of me, photographs of different men wearing different faces. Expressions, he would correct me. But they were different faces. He would ask me to tell him what they were feeling but I never knew how. How to tell, how to know, what was really going on.

But I practiced and got better. I would watch Nina. She would look into her camera and smile so widely. She was happy; she loved the people she was speaking to. But they were, are, just strangers. Faces she cannot even see. I'm her sister. Yet she looks at me with a face I cannot read.

I never know what Nina wants.

Then I hear it. The gentle tap on the large kitchen window. I bolt out of my seat to fling it open before Dad or Nina even notice. I could hear her knuckles graze the glass before the knock even happened.

Keedie is here.

She clambers into the kitchen, ducking through the window. I hug her. She's the only person I ever hug. She never grips me too tightly, she never tenses. She doesn't wear strong perfume that stings my nose, just a mild soap that smells like home.

"Hello, my favourite person." Her voice is all one colour, a beautiful molten gold.

I smile against her ribs. She asks me no questions. She lets go when I do.

"Nina, I might drop out of university and start influencing like you," Keedie falls into the chair next to mine and starts eating what is left of the pasta. "I can't stand anyone in my lectures, and the rooms are awful."

"Very funny," Nina is being sarcastic but she smiles very slightly. "What's wrong with the rooms?"

Keedie looks at me and grins. I instinctively grin back. "Bad lights."

I nod in full understanding.

"Oh, I see," Nina sips some more of her juice. "It's a little secret between you two."

Bad lights are the kind of lights that are so bright, they give people like me headaches. They hurt our eyes – they are visually loud.

Keedie is Nina's twin. But she is not like Nina. She is like me. Autistic, like me.

*

Keedie and I go walking by the Water of Leith after dinner. We enjoy the sound of our shoes crunching on the gravel path leading down to the muddy bank of the river. I reach out to touch the leaf of a tree which will soon turn a different colour and then die. I bawled when Mum first told me about the leaf on the tree but she explained that it's good and normal. That it doesn't hurt them to die.

"Miss Murphy shouted at me today." I kick a stone so it soars through the air and lands in the running water. "Because my handwriting was messy."

Keedie stops walking to glance at me. I know my face will be difficult for her to read. We step onto the bridge over the river. I have a handful of sticks that I'm ready to drop.

"She shouldn't have done that, Addie."

"She didn't read it. She said she couldn't."

"It's because of your motor skills," Keedie stops and gently takes my hands.

"Motor skills?"

"Our brain sends messages to our hands. It tells them what do to." She touches her finger to my palm and then my temple. "When you're… different, your processing is a little unique. The hands have a bit of trouble doing exactly what the brain wants. They're so busy getting the words exactly right, and in the right order, that they don't have time to get the writing perfect or pretty."

"Ok." I stop walking and absorb what Keedie has said.

"My handwriting is the same way." She nudges me and laughs. "That's why Nina won't let me sign Christmas cards from the two of us."

I laugh as a memory of Nina sitting by the fireplace last December with all of the holiday cards spread out in front of her appears in my head. She was very serious about the whole process, the wrapping as well.

"I use a laptop at university," Keedie adds. "It's much easier for me."

I nibble on my bottom lip. "I don't think Miss Murphy would like that."

"No," Keedie sighs. "If memory serves, she hates anything that might actually help someone."

"There's a new girl in our class this year," I change the conversation, something Mum says is important to do if you have nothing further to say. "She's from London."

"How exciting."

"I don't think she has any friends yet."

"Well," Keedie gestures for me to start dropping my sticks over the edge of the bridge. "Maybe you should be her friend."

"If she likes the library," I drop my first stick, and watch the splash as it hits the water, "then that would be fine."

"What about Jenna?"

"She sits with Emily now. I don't think Emily likes me."

I can tell Keedie these things. If I told Mum or Nina, they would say that I was being silly and that I should just sit with them at lunch and be friends with both of them.

Just be nice and friendly. Of course she wants to be your friend, too.

Keedie knows that it is not that simple. That first impressions are horrible. That making new friends is not easy. I can see the whispers, the stares and the giggles. And I know that they are not good things.

"Well then, you should definitely be friends with this new girl then," Keedie says.

I nod. Something has changed in the last few years. It used to be easy to go up to someone in the playground and ask to play. Now, people sit in tight little groups and they like to talk instead of play.

I miss the playing.

"You know," Keedie pushes her golden hair out of her face. "I haven't told anyone at uni that I'm autistic."

I stare up at her. She's so tall, with legs that seem longer than my whole body. I'm always looking up at her. "Why not?"

Keedie is never afraid to talk about being autistic. She is, as Dad says, "loud and proud". She was diagnosed around the same age that I was, between nine and ten. Mum said Nina would do everything as expected; she walked and talked quickly, she liked most foods, she did fine in school. Keedie didn't speak until she was five. She jokingly says that it was because she had nothing to say. She struggled with other children, she fought with teachers, she had difficulty controlling her emotions. She would only take part in school if she was engaged or interested. Mum says she would sometimes get a phone call from the school telling her that Keedie had just walked out of a maths lesson.

I have Keedie to explain everything to me. To tell me why my handwriting is bad, why loud noises and bright colours make my mind catch fire.

She had no one to tell her.

"Most people still don't understand, Addie."

"But," I get the sudden urge to stim, the conversation feels too loaded. "Won't it be harder masking full-time?"

Stimming is something I do when I'm overwhelmed. My hands fizz and flap, my limbs become restless. I sometimes feel the urge to pat the back of my head. There can be good stimming, there can be bad stimming, but a lot of the time I have to hide it. Masking is when we have to pass as a neurotypical person, as someone who is not like us. We have to ignore the need to stim, self-soothe and we have to make firm eye contact. Keedie told me it's like when superheroes have to pretend that they're regular people.

"Ah, I'm getting pretty good at it now," Keedie winks at me, her big green eyes bright and difficult for me to read.

People aren't like books. A familiar book is always the same, always comforting and full of the same words and pictures. A familiar person can be new and challenging, no matter how many times you try to read them.

As we make our way back home, Keedie stops. "Want to run down the hill?"

"Yes!" I shout.

So we run. My hands flap freely and joyfully, able to stim without anyone telling my not to. Keedie whoops and sings. We reach the bottom, breathless and exhilarated. Keedie gives me the quickest hug from behind and we head home in the dim September light.

Chapter Three

"Hi, Jenna."

Everyone is waiting outside of the classroom to go in, so I decide to approach Jenna. We've been friends since nursery, and she's even stayed over at my house. But I haven't seen her at all over the summer and she has spent every minute of term so far with Emily.

"Hi, Addie."

She avoids looking at me. I don't mind, because sometimes I don't like to look at people. I especially don't like to look at people if I'm trying to say something important. Emily is looking at me though. She makes sure that I see her look me up and down. She then slips her arm through Jenna's.

"Can we help you with something?" Emily says it slowly and loudly, tilting her head to one side like a German Shepherd. I'm not sure why she always speaks so slowly to me, I actually prefer fast talking.

"Do you want to have lunch on the grass with me today?"

I ask both of them, even though I don't really know Emily.

The playground isn't very big, and the boys take up a lot of space playing football, but there is a patch of grass by the bicycle shed where it can be quieter and more relaxing.

"Um," Jenna glances at Emily and fidgets, shifting her weight from one foot to the other.

"No," Emily answers for her, smiling a nasty smile. "She doesn't. She doesn't want to have lunch with you, Addie. No one does."

"I do."

All three of us turn. Audrey, the new girl, is standing a few feet away and has obviously been watching the whole conversation. She is tall for our age, like Keedie, and has black hair and dark eyes.

"Well," Emily turns to Audrey but she doesn't seem as confident now as she was a moment ago, "nobody asked you. Nobody was talking to you."

"Yeah, you're right," Audrey responds, moving past Emily and looking her up and down — exactly like Emily had done to me. "Nobody was talking."

She moves into the classroom as the bell goes and Jenna makes a noise in the back of her throat. "She's calling you a nobody, Em."

Emily's whole face has gone pink and I feel a little sorry for her. Whenever I feel sorry or sad for people that I don't know very well, I never know what to say to them. So I just slide by the two of them and head into the classroom. Audrey looks up from her seat as I pass and gives me a nod. I don't know what to do so I nod back.

As everyone files into their seats, Miss Murphy arrives with a mug of hot tea. I watch her gulp some of it down and shiver. Hot liquids are terrible on my tongue. Always too scorching, always the wrong texture.

"I think we're going to have fun today," she tells us, as she leans against her desk. "We've got a good project to work on in the lead up to Halloween. Now, if you remember last week, I told you that we would be studying Old Edinburgh, as proud residents of the good city."

I don't understand people in this village. We live a good way out of Edinburgh and yet they all insist on pretending that we don't. Nina does it too. She tells her followers about how she lives in an Edinburgh townhouse. In fact, we live in a Juniper semi-detached house with only one bathroom between five people. Juniper is a pretty village, though. Small, with a few houses, a church, our school, one supermarket, one dentist, one doctor, one funeral parlour and the bank.

Why everyone is desperate to be from Edinburgh is beyond me.

"Now, can any one of you tell me," she pauses for a moment and looks steadily around the classroom, "what might have got you dunked in the Nor' Loch back in the old days of Edinburgh?"

I know that the Princes Street Gardens in Edinburgh were once a loch, but this is the first I have heard about dunking.

It seems I am not alone, nobody answers Miss Murphy.

"Jenna?"

Jenna, who was whispering with Emily, glances up like a startled rabbit. "Um…"

"Oh, never mind," Miss Murphy moves to the board and begins to draw. She draws a woman and as soon as she begins to add a pointed hat, many of us cry out, "WITCH!"

"Yes! In old Edinburgh, and many other parts of Scotland and the world, you could be tried and executed for being a witch."

I stare at Miss Murphy and feel all of the air in the room disappear. I look around at my classmates, and they all look very entertained. But I feel like my whole world has been shaken and turned upside down. Witches! Real witches! Here, in Scotland. It seems too exciting, too wonderful to be true.

I'm standing before I even realise it. "Real witches, Miss?" I stare at her imploringly, desperate to hear more.

"Sit down, Adeline."

"Of course not real witches, stupid," Emily says loudly, leaning across her desk to glare at me.

Miss Murphy once told one of the boys off for calling another boy "stupid", but she doesn't tell Emily off.

"Emily is right," Miss Murphy goes back to the lesson as I shakily sit down. "They of course could not have been real witches; such things do not exist."

"Then why were they tried and executed?" I ask the question without thinking, every nerve on my body alive and impatient to know everything. When I am interested in a subject, I have to know everything about it immediately. I can't help it. Information never seems to come fast enough.

"Adeline, I won't have you shouting out like this," Miss Murphy snaps. "Be quiet."

My hands are wringing. She isn't explaining quickly enough for my wired mind.

"People could be accused of witchcraft for all kinds of reasons. Something as small as being left-handed could be enough to cause suspicion. Is anyone here left-handed?"

Audrey, the new girl, raises her hand.

"Then you," Miss Murphy points at Audrey with her pen, "might have been accused of being a witch, my girl."

Audrey does not look entirely thrilled by this notion. I have a thousand burning questions and I wriggle in my seat, trying to stay on top of them all.

"It is said that witches were dunked in the Nor' Loch. Their thumbs and toes were tied together and they were tossed into the water! If they floated, they were guilty of witchcraft. If they drowned, they were innocent. Guilty witches were removed from the loch and taken to Castlehill to be burned or hanged."

"But then they couldn't win!" Miss Murphy rolls her eyes at my interruption but I continue, "There's no way to survive that."

"No," Miss Murphy concedes. "It was a tricky way of trying people."

I feel... angry. The unfairness of it sits in my stomach like a stone. I imagine women being frightened and alone as they are thrown into the cold water. The harsh splash, the possibility of floating and facing even more pain.

"Some were even tortured. And some of the women tried for witchcraft in Scotland came from this very village!"

I look around at the others. Their faces are difficult for me to read on a normal day, but now I cannot understand why they are not as distressed as I am. My hands are tremoring and begging to be used, so I clutch my thesaurus as tightly as possible to give them something to grip.

"The only way for the women in this village to be safe was for them to be as inconspicuous as possible."

"What does that mean?" Emily asks.

I want to tell her it means being ordinary and unremarkable but I don't. I'm too overstimulated. My legs just want to run to the library and read as much about this as possible, and then dash out of the school to run and find Keedie.

"Yes, indeed," Miss Murphy is smirking at all of us. "Being different meant you would probably end up being tried and found guilty."

"Addie would have been burned then," Emily says, sniggering.

The rest of the class laugh, and Miss Murphy joins in. I hardly hear them. I'm visualising the books I want to start reading.

"Did lots of women in Juniper die, Miss?" I ask, hovering above my seat. Practically levitating.

"Exact numbers are not known," Miss Murphy

answers, her smile gone. "But records suggest there were at least fifty, not only from Juniper, but the surrounding villages."

My brain flashes back to when there was a car crash on the main road leading into Juniper. People left photographs of the victim, and flowers. It's still there now, a year on. I also think of the war cenotaph with my great-grandfather's name on it. The only thing I have of him. My brain is sending images to me as quickly as possible and together they form a question.

"Is there a," my brain works quickly to find the correct word to use, "memorial for the witches in Juniper?"

"Of course not," Miss Murphy shakes her head and fixes me with a stern look. "What a waste of time that would be."

"But if that many women were killed——"

"Enough. You've disrupted this lesson enough."

She carries on while my mind wanders to the library. I can feel Audrey watching me and she is still doing so when the bell for lunch rings and I fly out of my seat.

*

"What's wrong, Addie, you look a little flushed?"

"Nothing's wrong," I tell Mr Allison as I burst into the library. "I need all of the books on witches, please."

"All the books!" Mr Allison laughs and crosses his arms, heading over to the Story-time Corner.

"No, not fiction," I add, hurrying to stand beside him. "Textbooks. On the Scottish Witch Trials."

"Oh, I see," he says, stepping back and surveying the whole room. "I think I can get you a couple. Has Miss Murphy been telling you all about it?"

"Not all about it," I admit, grimly. "Just a little bit about it."

"And if I know you," Mr Allison says while picking out a large reference book from the shelf, "you're not going to be happy until you've understood everything about it."

I let him hand me the books he's selected, and I head to a table. Mr Allison never makes fun of my behaviour. He never rolls his eyes or questions me. He understands.

"How are the sharks coming along?" he asks, while I lay out my new books.

"Good," I reply, placing my lunchbox on the table. "No Great White Shark has ever survived captivity. They die almost instantly."

"Oh," Mr Allison frowns gently. "That's not very good."

"It is, actually," I tell him. "It means humans have stopped trying to capture them. They can just be free."

"I suppose it's not much fun in captivity."

I shake my head. "Not fun at all."

"You remember to actually eat your lunch now, Addie."

Sometimes I read so intently, I forget to eat. He's obviously taken notice.

Mr Allison doesn't mind me eating my lunch in the library, as long as I am tidy, so I carefully chew my chicken and mayo sandwich on brown bread as I pour over an Eyewitness textbook about Edinburgh. As I'm reading a certain chapter, another lunchbox lands next to mine and a person appears in my vision.

Audrey.

"Are you looking up the witch trials?" she asks. She sounds as if she genuinely wants to know. But sometimes other kids sound nice but are actually being mean. I am cautious.

"Yes," I reply. "Miss Murphy doesn't explain things enough. I want to understand."

"I'm sorry people said those horrible things in the classroom."

Her accent is different to all of ours. Less sharp and spiky. But it also doesn't sound like the English people who read the news on television.

I wave away her apology. "It's okay. They always say things like that."

I frantically turn the page to devour the next.

"Can I help you research?"

I glance up and try to read her face. My brain is a little frantic to mask properly at the moment. But she seems well-meaning. "Okay."

She smiles, unpacks her lunch and moves her seat a little closer in order to read. We sit together and read in silence.

Chapter Four

"Why on earth are we here?"

Mum, Dad, Keedie and I are sitting in the third row of the Juniper village hall as people file in for the bimonthly committee meeting. I lied about the starting time so that we would be early. Mum and Dad are not impressed.

Nina has just arrived, her face almost entirely concealed by a knitted scarf. Her eyes look baffled. She shuffles down the row to sit next to Keedie.

"We are here," Keedie answers her, "because Addie wants to propose something to the committee."

Nina looks at me and then leans across to look at Mum and Dad who are on my other side. "What?"

"Don't ask us," Mum says, still tired after her nursing shift and trying not to yawn. "Addie wouldn't tell us. We were all marched here after dinner."

I watch the committee members take their seats, check their watches and shake each other's hands. There are five men and one woman, all my grandparents' age.

"Addie," Nina is using her grown-up voice with me. "This isn't something silly, is it?"

"Can't be sillier than talking about make-up to a camera for a living," Keedie says quietly, not looking at either of us.

I'm switched on enough to catch a flash of hurt on Nina's face before she settles on an eye roll. I feel bad for her, I don't think her vlogging is silly. I think she's good at it and it seems to make lots of people happy.

"It's not silly, Nina," I tell her, trying to make my voice sound calm.

"This is exactly what Mum and I want to be doing after a really long work day," Dad says jokingly. Mum laughs. I even smile a little, despite my nerves.

As the last of the village attendees sit in their chairs, Mr Macintosh takes his place at the head of the committee table. I don't know the names of the other members, I only know Mr Macintosh because he works at the school.

The meeting begins and I am slightly dismayed at how long it takes to get to "new business". The members talk about a change in the bus timetable, plans for roadworks and then he finally opens the floor to the villagers. And me.

Several hands shoot up all at once, mine included, and a collective groan ripples throughout the room. Mr Macintosh, however, is delighted at the number of people wanting to speak and he goes straight for Lisa McLaren in the front row. The mother of three who lives four doors down from us rises to her feet with great importance.

"There needs to be a curfew on youths at the park."

Some bemused murmurings follow her opening statement and I hear Keedie let out a long sigh. I glance over and smile at her expression. Her eyes are crossed and she is pretending to slip down and fall out of her chair. Nina grabs her elbow and throws her a look.

"They loiter," Lisa goes on without invitation. "They smoke, they start fires and they're generally loud and incredibly threatening. I propose a curfew be set for the park so as people between the ages of ten and eighteen are not permitted to gather there."

"So what?" Keedie calls out before Nina can stop her. "You're going to have a bouncer at the swings?"

Disapproving eyes swivel our way while Mum and Nina shush her, and Dad and I laugh.

"The keeper of the park should be permitted to call the police on anyone loitering or acting suspiciously," Lisa adds, ignoring Keedie and staring down the assembly panel with birdlike intensity.

"I don't think we can remove the children unless they're explicitly breaking the law, Lisa," Mr Macintosh says, looking uncomfortable. "But we can certainly look into more patrols of the park after dark. Next?"

Dismissed, Lisa sits down with a look of utter dissatisfaction. Mr Laird rises in her place, eyes slightly wild and moustache aquiver.

"The geese," he booms, "at Juniper Pond are demonic."

There are some groans, but a couple of "ayes".

"What do you propose we do about them, Robert?" Mr Macintosh asks, sounding as tired as Mum.

"Eat them!"

"No. Next?"

A written request from the village minister is read aloud, kindly asking that the models posing for the Thursday life drawing classes please wait until the room has been cleared of other church visitors before disrobing.

"Aye, ask him to turn the heating on then," grumbles someone from the back.

Old Ms Flaherty asks that the village's one and only bus stop be moved so that it is further away from the bank and then there is a sudden moment of stillness amongst the hall of villagers.

Keedie nudges me and I seize my chance, leaping to my feet and declaring, "There should be a new village memorial."

Macintosh's eyes close in exhausted trepidation for a moment before he gestures for me to continue.

"This village," I am aware of the whole room watching and listening but it is too late to stop now, "executed more women for the crimes of "witchcraft" than any other in the lowlands of Scotland. Countless tortured and dead with no hint of a fair and just trial. No burial. No remembrance."

There is silence. My mouth is dry.

"And what exactly is it that you want?" one of the committee members asks, and I cannot see the colours in his tone.

"A memorial. A plaque or a statue that commemorates the people that were unjustly sentenced to death."

There is more silence. And then some murmuring.

"I don't think," Mr Macintosh finally speaks, but he won't look at me, "that a memorial for some witches would be a good addition to the village. We have a shot at becoming a tourist spot, young lady, and we don't want anything that might tarnish the village reputation."

"Are you kidding?" Keedie is suddenly by my side and speaking loudly and clearly. "People love witches! Also, this village could do with a bit more to say for itself. We have that plaque by the park which says Bonnie Prince Charlie rode through with his soldiers. Actually, it says he might have come through here. If that warrants a bloody plaque, and being constantly talked about, then why doesn't this?"

"Bonnie Prince Charlie did come through here!" someone at the back yells, sounding very defensive.

"Oh, really, were you there?" Keedie shouts back.

Mum and Nina are both hissing at her to sit back down.

"I…" my dry, scratchy throat and my nerves make it difficult to speak. "I think it would be a nice thing to do, sir. If… if I were one of those witches, I would want somebody to remember me."

Keedie briefly squeezes my hand.

"I'm sorry, young lady," Mr Macintosh shakes his head. "It's nice to see a young person so politically engaged but it's a "no" from this assembly."

Another door before me. It was slightly ajar. Now it's closed.

*

"It's important to try your best, even if the answer is a no, Addie," Dad tells me as we arrive home after the meeting.

I say nothing.

"Oh, Ads." Mum strokes my hair. "Don't be upset. You can try again in a few weeks."

"She's not upset," Keedie says, hanging her coat up. "She's resigned. That's what happens when you get constantly treated like dirt in this place."

"Oi!" Mum's tone is dark and stormy. "Enough of that."

"It's true," Keedie says. Her face is an open book. She is angry and upset. "This village is stuck in the dark ages." She turns to me. "Addie, I thought you were amazing. Staying so calm and masking so well when that stupid light was flickering like mad."

Of course Keedie had noticed. Near the end of the evening, a ceiling light kept going on and off, each time causing my nerves to spark and my eyes to sting. It wasn't bothering any of the people around me. But to me, it was like a needle poking my eyelid.

Mum and Dad go to sit in the living room with some wine. Keedie goes to have a shower, and I am walking upstairs when Nina calls my name. I turn.

"Do you want to be in one of my videos?"

I had never thought about it. Nina makes videos about make-up and hair, things that I know I may never be interested in. But she looks so open for once, I don't want to say no.

"Okay."

We sit in front of her camera, which she speaks to like a friend. She introduces me.

"This is my little sister, Addie. She's autistic and not very interested in beauty." She makes a performative face for the camera, though I'm not sure what it means. "So I'll be giving her a little crash course today."

She scoots her seat closer to mine and snatches up a brush.

"I'm just going to do your hair quickly, so it's out of your face," she says.

My hair is long, like hers. Light brown with gold, Mum says. Nina brushes efficiently, but gently. For the longest time, I hated having my hair washed and brushed. Hated the sensation. Mum and Dad didn't know what to do. But Nina had always been so good with hair, she would carefully wash mine twice a week and put it into two French braids.

She was the only one who knew what to do.

"Do you want to talk about your autism for the viewers, Addie?" she asks me.

"Uh," I glance at the camera lens. "Not really."

"Ok," she sighs. "So we'll get started with some cosmetics then..."

"Nina?"

"Yes?"

"Do you think Keedie is okay?"

Nina sighs heavily. "I'll have to cut all this out, Addie, just try to talk about what we're doing."

"But do you?"

"University is a big change," she acknowledges, sorting through brushes. "She's just going to be a bit more tired, a bit more worn out."

"Is that why you decided not to go to uni?"

She hesitates over her many little bottles of concealer. "Well, I do this for work, Addie."

Nina gets really upset when people say her vlogging isn't really a job so I don't say anything else. She takes a deep breath and then her face transforms once more into a bright and happy smile.

"I'm going to swatch some concealer and then start under Addie's eyes."

She starts.

She talks to both the camera and me as she puts colours on my eyelids and cheeks. It's awful. It feels so uncomfortable, like paint. But she's so close to me and she's being so calm and nice. I don't want to ruin it, so I sit still and let her do it.

I'm happy she wants to be near me. So I let it all go.

Chapter Five

All I can think about are the witches.

I walk through the Juniper woods and pretend that I have magical powers. I cast spells on the trees and on the water. My large headphones are playing music while I spin and stim through the trees. I wonder if any of the witches walked this path. If they tried to escape into these woods to avoid capture.

Keedie is walking behind me laughing. I pretend to cast a spell upon her and she collapses onto the muddy path. I scream in delight.

She gets up and we walk the trail, my headphones resting on my shoulders.

"Have you told the people at university that you're autistic?"

"Um," Keedie sniffs and admires the trees over our heads. "Not yet. I don't think I need to."

"But you always said it's important to be open and proud about it."

"And I am proud," Keedie says, and I can tell she is being picky about her words. "But it wasn't easy at school for me, Addie. I had a tough time sometimes with bullies."

"Are there bullies at universities?"

"Well, sort of." She picks a leaf from a tree and wraps her hand around it. "Bullies don't go away after primary school, Addie. Grown-ups can be bullies, too."

One of my earliest memories was from when I was four and we had a horrible childminder. Mum and Dad were working different schedules, and Mrs Craig would come over for some evenings. Mum said she chose her because of her experience as a social worker.

Keedie was my age then and having a difficult time. Little things could trigger panic attacks and meltdowns. After Mum would leave for her shift, Mrs Craig's entire personality would change. She would snarl at everything Keedie said and call her a spoiled brat. One evening, Keedie was having trouble with the dinner Mrs Craig had made. I remember disliking it too. Even Nina was grappling with it and Nina never likes to displease grown-ups.

When Keedie reached a stage of no longer being able to stomach it, Mrs Craig lost it. She threw a plate and dived at Keedie.

And then something broke inside of my sister.

She howled. I still remember the sound. Screaming, crying and beating her own head. It was like she was trying to knock all of the horrible names she had been called out of her mind. Mrs Craig sprang into action, cursing Keedie all the while, and using her considerable weight to restrain my sister. She pinned Keedie's wrists to the ground and got right in her face.

"Stop!" Nina cried, looking more afraid than I had ever seen her. Memories from so long ago can be difficult sometimes, but this one is as clear as a film scene in my head. I remember the feelings as vividly as the look of contorted pain and terror on Keedie's face.

"Stop this right now, you little animal," hissed Mrs Craig. She didn't look angry though. She looked like she was enjoying it.

Then I remember the red feeling. The hot rush, the painful hammering of my heart.

I flew at her.

My whole body hit her back with the force of a train and I sank my teeth into her fleshy shoulder. She yelped and screeched, letting go of Keedie to try and break free from my bite. Keedie's whole body was convulsing with sobs.

If our neighbour, Jackie, hadn't come banging on the door at that moment, Keedie and Nina say they don't know what might have happened. Mum and Dad were called, Jackie never taking her eyes away from Mrs Craig.

I was immediately taken away from the entire scene when our parents came home. I remember there was shouting but Nina was covering my ears. She lay next to me in bed, whispering nonsense to try and distract me.

Keedie didn't come out of her room for days.

Now, I look up at my sister. She is beautiful. Her hair is long and magical-looking, the autumn sun showing off the golden blonde streaks. She is my reliable older sister. I can't connect that trembling child to this confident person.

I know if anyone tried to hurt Keedie, even now, I would probably still try to bite them.

"Tell me more about your witches."

She knows that getting me started on one of my obsessions is always a good idea.

"I read about one from Juniper called Maggie," I tell her, grabbing my own tree leaf to clutch. "They said that she was married to the devil."

Keedie laughs heartily at this. "What on earth was the devil doing in Scotland? Far too cold here, I would have thought."

"They all made up lies to try and find a good reason for calling them witches," I say bitterly.

"I know," Keedie says. "That's always the way."

"I don't think Maggie knew the right things to say," I

tell her. "There wasn't that much written about her in the book but they eventually forced her to admit to being a witch. Even though she wasn't."

Keedie smiles gently at me. "That's really sad, kid. Poor Maggie."

"Emily says I would have been burned for being a witch," I admit suddenly.

"Well, you know what," Keedie says crisply. "I think Emily sounds utterly rotten. I don't know what Jenna sees in her."

"She's more girly than me, I think," I say. "They do each other's hair and paint their nails and things." I crumple up my leaf. "I can't paint nails. Jenna made me try when she slept over and I made such a mess."

"Did Jenna ever want to do anything you wanted to do?"

I think about it. "I don't know. I did whatever she wanted."

Keedie stops me and points at a steady old tree at the end of the path, right by the bridge across the river. "See that tree?"

"Yes."

"Some people are like trees. The wind can blow and blow, they'll never move. They'll always be there."

I look up at her. She smiles and nods at the leaf in my hand.

"Now open up your hand."

I do.

"Hold it up."

I hold my hand up, the leaf resting on my palm. In seconds, the wind rushes and blows the entire thing away. I gasp.

"Jenna was a leaf, Addie," Keedie says gently. "You're a tree."

I screw my face up trying to make sense of what she's saying. She seems mysterious to me these days. A little out of my reach. I slip my hand into hers. I won't do it for long, neither of us enjoy it after a while.

But for now it feels good to touch.

We walk back up the path to the village and, as we leave the woods and the trees, I spot Mr Macintosh leaving the bank. I'm calling his name before I can think to stop myself and I start to run. Keedie follows, calling my name.

Mr Macintosh stares at me, looking slightly afraid. He looks over at Keedie, as if he's hoping she'll pull me away.

"You have to reconsider, Mr Macintosh."

"Reconsider what?" he says, glancing around. Perhaps hoping that another grown-up will come to his rescue.

"The memorial for the witches," I remind him.

"Oh," he scoffs and shakes his head. "This is such silliness, Adeline. And, quite honestly, I'm not sure who has put you up to this, but it's already been rejected."

"Put me up to it?"

He bends down so that we're level and then speaks very slowly, in the same voice that Emily uses. "Who put the idea in your head?"

"I did," I assure him.

He laughs, but it's not a nice laugh. He straightens and begins to walk towards his car. "It's cruel to use your sister for your antics, Keedie."

Baffled, I turn to look at my sister. She's staring daggers at Mr Macintosh.

"But it's my idea, Mr Macintosh," I call after him. "We're learning about it at school."

"Aye, sure," he says, shutting the door and starting the engine.

I open my mouth to say something more but Keedie places a hand on my arm. "Don't, Addie. He wants to believe his small-minded nonsense, let him."

"But I don't understand."

"When grown-ups don't like what we have to say, they blame our autism and say we don't know our own minds." She exhales and shrugs. "It was textbook when I was at that rubbish school.

Constantly accused of copying. They couldn't believe the ideas were mine."

"But that's…" I feel the urge to stamp my foot but I push it down. "That makes me feel like the witches! Like we can't win."

"I know."

I watch the little car drive away and I blow out a large puff of air. "I'm going to the next village hall meeting to bring it up again."

When Keedie doesn't respond, I turn to look up at her. She's smiling.

"I think that's a fabulous idea."

Chapter Six

"You read a lot, don't you?"

Audrey and I are walking home from school. It's a new routine. It took a little getting used to, my walk to and from school was my time to prepare for the chaos of a busy day. But Audrey isn't overly talkative and doesn't bombard me with questions, so I don't mind so much.

"I'm reading about this woman, Maggie. She used to live here in Juniper. She was one of the 'witches'."

"Maggie?"

"Yeah. They said she was a witch, but she wasn't really."

"I can't believe you do extra work outside of school," Audrey laughs.

"I don't always," I admit. "Only if I find it interesting. When I don't find something interesting, my brain switches off."

"Yeah, I can see it sometimes," Audrey says. "When Murphy was talking about long division, I could see you staring out of the window."

I wrinkle my nose. "I can't help it, I swear."

"But then you know so much about all of these

witches," she points out. "I didn't do any reading on Maggie, that's for sure."

"My sister says my brain is like a computer," I explain. "It starts with no information and then just collects more and more, it never stops."

"Are all brains like that?"

"Maybe. But mine crashes every time it gets overused."

We walk without talking for a little before Audrey speaks softly. "So… what's wrong with you?"

I hesitate, trying to work out if she's being mean or not.

"I found your sister's video," she says. "She was doing your make-up."

"I'm autistic," I finally say, looking up at the cloudy Scottish sky. October is bringing the cold and the rain. The wind hits the trees on our street with incredible force, I don't know how they stand it.

"What's that?"

"It's a neurological condition," I touch my temple. "Meaning, it's a difference in the brain. It's a spectrum. Some people have it and don't speak at all. And some have it and talk a lot."

"Like you."

"Yeah."

"And," Audrey is trying to understand, I can tell, "what does it do to you?"

"I… feel things a bit more. Sounds, sights. I can hear people down the street without straining. I can see tiny details in things. Things other people can't. I process things differently. And sometimes," I kick a stone on the pavement, "sometimes, it's really difficult for me to read people's faces. If they're not being honest with their faces, I sometimes don't understand."

"Okay."

She doesn't ask me anything more about it. It isn't until I reach home that I realise Jenna never wanted to know about being autistic.

I've brought home two new books from the library. One about sharks and another about witches. I run inside the house and head for the kitchen. However, Nina is sitting at the table in tears.

I stop. Tears are always trouble. Sometimes people cry because they are happy, which is endlessly confusing. But Nina really doesn't seem happy. Also, when she realises that it's me, she fiercely wipes her eyes.

"What's happened?" I croak.

She suddenly glances over my shoulder and I turn to see Keedie. She has red eyes too and looks angry.

"Keedie and I are having a grown-up conversation, Addie." Nina moves to pour some water. "Go upstairs and read your book, please."

I look up at Keedie. She tries to smile but she isn't able to lie with her expressions. She still looks angry and sad.

I pretend to go up to my room, but I hide on the stairs. My hearing is good enough, I can make out every word. Even with the kitchen door almost closed.

"You exposed her to monsters, Nina."

"Don't be so melodramatic, Keedie, I disabled the comments. They're gone now."

"Thought you'd show off your troubled little sister," Keedie is spitting out her words. "Thought you would get internet brownie points for daring to be nice to a disabled child."

"That disabled child is my sister, too," Nina yells. "Not just yours!"

"It's not a competition! She's a person, not a prop. She's vulnerable and you put her on the internet for all the dregs of humanity to point and stare at."

"She's functioning—don't make that face, it's a perfectly appropriate medical term—she's functioning and I thought people might like to see that. She has it mild, Keedie. Like you."

"It's mild to you!" Keedie shouts and I flinch, not used to hearing her raise her voice. "It's mild to you and every other heartless soul in this village, Nina, it's not mild to me. It's not mild to Addie! It's mild to you because we make it so, at great personal cost!"

"Oh, stop it."

"You know, Nina," I can hear Keedie slamming a drawer, "she is so uncomfortable in that video. If you actually knew her, you would have seen that. She's only doing it to please you."

There is silence for a bit. I feel like I'm trapped in a box.

"I deleted the comments," Nina finally says quietly. "Leave it alone now."

I hear rustling and movement before Keedie replies, "You owe her an apology."

It's clear that they are finished with their argument, as Keedie goes into the living room and puts music on. I sneak into Mum and Dad's room and load up their old computer in the corner. I find Nina's channel. I find the video. It's true, she has disabled the comments. But the website links to a "reply video".

I get one minute into a woman Mum's age talking about how I am cursed and a "modern tragedy" before I can't bear it anymore. I read the comments beneath the woman's words. People agree. They use words Mum and Dad say we should never, ever use. Some say I can't really be autistic if I can speak.

I close the page and wish, like how Nina deleted all of her comments, that I could delete these from my memory. It's so confusing. To be too much for some people and not enough for everyone else.

Their words are still burning my brain when Keedie comes into my bedroom to check on me.

"I'm guessing your magic hearing picked up some of the arguing," she says, putting a plate of chocolate biscuits on the table by my bed. "I'm sorry."

I'm on the bed, my back to her. "I wish I was like everybody else."

"No, you don't," she says instantly. "No, Addie. Other people's minds are small. Your mind is enormous. It has room for everything and everyone. You don't want to be like other people."

"How would you know, you're like me," I point out, my eyes stinging. "You're not normal either."

There is a pause.

"Addie," she sounds sad. "Your brain is why you can write your stories. All of your really amazing stories!"

"Miss Murphy tore my story apart!"

Silence. Then, "She did what?"

"She ripped up my shark story. In front of everyone."

"Addie, why didn't you tell us? She can't do that, she can't humiliate you like that."

"Well, she did." I don't know why I'm crying. "And I'm so tired."

She sighs. "I know, kid. I am, too."

I say nothing more. When she leaves, I pull out my shark book and stroke its polished pages. A basking shark with its incredible mouth wide open. A whale shark, so large and frightening and yet completely harmless. I close my eyes and wish so hard to disappear and reappear in the deep blue ocean, able to swim for miles and miles without having to face another living creature.

A tear drops and lands on the face of a zebra shark. I quickly wipe it away. No horrible, awful, rubbish day is worth damaging a library book.

Chapter Seven

School trips are enormous gambles for me.

While the idea of seeing new places, and learning new information can seem irresistible, the reality of classmates pushing and shoving, loud traffic noises and an unfamiliar routine often dampens the day.

Luckily, today's journey does not involve a minibus or train. We are simply walking from the school to the Water of Leith. Miss Murphy tells us to grab a partner and stay in two neat lines.

"I'm going with Jenna," Emily says, her face right up close to my own. "My best friend."

I lean back, drawing myself away from her closeness. "I can smell your breakfast, Emily."

Audrey laughs heartily and stands next to me at the back of the line, while Emily flounces off. "That was funny."

"I didn't mean it to be funny," I tell her truthfully. "I have," I flick through my mental thesaurus, "acute senses."

"Cute senses?"

"Acute."

"What does that mean?"

"Like… really sharp senses. They pick things up easily. I could smell her apple juice."

Audrey is looking at me with a half-smile. "You're quite weird, Addie."

Our lines begin to move. I don't deny her statement. I know she means it in a good way.

A lot of other people don't.

We all follow Miss Murphy out of the playground, leaving the school behind, and head into the village. The woods are on the other side of Juniper, with a steep path leading down to the river.

Waiting for us at the school gates is a man who looks to be only a few years older than Nina and Keedie. He is wearing wellies and is waving very enthusiastically at us.

"Children," Miss Murphy does not sound quite as eager as this man looks. "This is Mr Patterson. He is completing his PhD at Edinburgh university and is going to give us a tour today."

"What's a PhD?" Audrey whispers.

"I don't know."

"Penguins Having Dinner."

Emily and Jenna casts glances back at the two of us, our laughter drawing their attention. Emily screws up her face and makes a noise of derision.

Jenna looks surprised, her eyes flickering over Audrey. Assessing her.

"Hello!" Mr Patterson addresses us and it is immediately obvious that he is not used to children. "Are we excited to learn about witches?"

My brain goes from sitting comfortably in a chair to frantically putting its shoes on. Desperate, animated and ready.

"Yes!" I call out.

Some people snigger but Mr Patterson looks amused.

After researching the witches myself, I discovered that the dunking trials Miss Murphy mentioned were not used very often, and were more popular in Europe. So I want to find out what really happened to witches here in Juniper. Keedie told me to tell Miss Murphy that she was misinformed and "talking crud", but Mum snapped at her. She told me strictly not to do that.

"Well, our first stop of the trip will be the Water of Leith, where we will visit the Old Witch Tree."

"Quick march!" Miss Murphy signals for us to follow her and Mr Patterson down to the woods and the riverside.

The tall trees block out what little sun there is in September. The ground is slightly muddy from a rainstorm during the night.

I try to perfectly fit my feet in the footprints left behind by the children in front of me.

I don't fit.

Miss Murphy and Mr Patterson stop at a stocky tree with thick, gnarly branches. They wait for us to all gather around.

"All right, children," Mr Patterson splays out his arms and looks into all of our faces, some bored and some curious. "I need us all to try and imagine this spot, this river and this path and all of these trees, I need you to imagine it hundreds of years ago."

I can immediately. No graffiti on the old crumbling walls. No plastic bags caught on the occasional tree. A darker, colder Juniper. Instead of car engines and the insistent beep of the pedestrian crossing, the faint sound of horses' hooves. Old paper mills.

"Now, hundreds of years ago, people lived in Juniper just like all of you. Farmers, millers and their families. The local church, or kirk, were the main authority in the village here. They made the important decisions, they controlled the running of Juniper. And they were the ones people went to if they knew of a witch."

He looks out eagerly at us all, eyes gleaming. "Do any of you know how to spot a witch?"

A few hands shoot up. He points to Alfie, one of the boys.

"They were old and ugly and rude."

"Well," Mr Patterson looks slightly taken aback. "I don't—maybe! Maybe, some of them. But that's actually a trick question. Because there was no way of spotting a witch. There were no firm rules."

He places a hand on the branch of the old tree behind him.

"There was a woman named Jean. Jean was known throughout Juniper for keeping to herself. She was a mutterer, a loner and had no family. While she usually kept away from other villagers, she one day found herself involved in a strong disagreement with one of her neighbours. In her anger as they fought, she cursed him. Who knows what a curse is?"

"Swearing?"

"Not quite, Jamie, but good try," Miss Murphy tells the boy with a wide smile.

"A curse," Mr Patterson continues, "is like an evil spell. It's when someone calls down a higher power, or magical force, to harm another person. Now, in the case of Jean, she was just angry; Cursed her neighbour out of anger and thought nothing more of it."

I try to imagine Jean. Tired and sullen, just wanting to be left alone. I can see people deliberately stepping into her path, forty years of being told to smile, to be pleasant.

"Curses aren't real though," Emily pipes up. "Magic isn't real."

"Well, we think that now," Miss Murphy says cordially, nodding her head. "But hundreds of years ago, people believed all sorts of different things."

"And Jean's neighbours became very afraid," Mr Patterson adds, desperate to continue his storytelling. "They went inside and fretted all night about the strange woman who had pointed her finger and perhaps hexed them. They told all of their friends in Juniper. And, eventually, the news reached the elders at the kirk."

I shiver.

"Now, if you were accused of being a witch, you would be put on trial. Juniper conducted many kirk sessions, where witches were interrogated and evidence was put forward by accusers and witnesses. However... legally, they were not permitted to execute witches. That fell to Edinburgh. But!"

He pauses. I am clinging to his every word, my eyes scanning his face for any giveaways that will complete the story for me.

"But," he seems thrilled to have our rapt attention, "vigilante justice was popular in Juniper. Who can tell me what that means?"

I know the answer but I don't want people looking at me right now. It feels strange to have all of my classmates in the woods that Keedie and I often walk in. A crowd in the woods seems unnatural.

"It's," Audrey begins to answer, "I think it's when people take the law into their own hands."

"You're absolutely right!" Mr Patterson is beaming at her. "So Jean's neighbours, days after the curse, found one of their animals dead. Of course, cattle die for all sorts of reasons. But they immediately suspected that it was because of Jean. That she was the one who had caused the cow to die."

The tale is setting my imagination on fire. I can see everyone he's describing, though I of course have never met them. It's a visual story in my head. Jean, washing her coarse hands and cleaning the worn sole of her boot, none the wiser to the cruel accusations and remarks that were being cast around in the village, to the powerful ears of the kirk elders.

Lies cast like spells. More powerful. More damaging.

"I want you all to hold Jean in your minds for a moment while we go on to another of Juniper's witches."

I blink. How can he leave the story unfinished?

"Now, the records about the Scottish witch trials are good but there will still be many witches whose full names and stories we will never know. We do know that the Lothian areas had the most witches," Miss Murphy tells us. "Juniper may not have had the authority to officially execute witches, but they certainly tracked many down, many who went on to Castlehill to be killed. Torture was also very popular, much more here than in England."

My hands are tremoring. The word torture is physical to me. I feel it circle around my wrists, tighten its grip on my throat.

"Mary was known to Juniper as a madwoman. She would beg for money all around the parish and was thought to be an imbecile. She was, judging by today's standards, quite mad. Quite in need of charity. But people were less understanding in those days, far less forgiving. The village collectively agreed that Mary was a witch."

I don't feel well.

"Now, Mary was not able to deny the accusation. She didn't understand what was happening. And this is where the vigilante justice comes into play!"

I start to edge away from the group. No one notices. My legs don't feel strong enough and my chest is tight.

"Both Mary and Jean went before the village council and were charged with witchcraft. Neighbours and villagers came forward to confirm that they had witnessed the women casting spells and endangering the village. However, when it was revealed that the women would go to Edinburgh for a full criminal trial, the village decided to take matters into their own hands."

"Why didn't they just say it was all made up?" asks Jenna, her face puzzled and a little disdainful.

When we were friends, Jenna would ask why a lot. Never how.

"Jean may well have done," Mr Patterson acknowledges. "But Mary was unable to grasp what was happening, what she was being accused of."

I sometimes have difficulty identifying feelings. Naming them. I can see the colours in them, can tell a bad emotion from a good one.

This is a bad feeling.

"Mary easily admitted to witchcraft after some interrogation. She even volunteered a birthmark which Juniper then declared was a mark of sorcery."

I think of Maggie. Possibly confused, admitting to being something that she was not. Maybe they told her she would get to go home if she just gave in and told them what they wanted to hear. Did they do the same to Mary?

"So then what happened?" Jenna asks the question. Hungrily.

"Mary's confession satisfied the mob of villagers, but they took it upon themselves to torture Jean until she did the same."

Some classmates make noises of disbelief and excitement. Mr Patterson goes into detail, describing crudely made thumb screws, whipping and other forms of torture. I move further and further away from the group, hoping that the sound of the gushing river will drown out his horrible words. Remove the ghostly, ghastly images from my head.

"At last, Jean could withstand no more. She confessed to being a witch."

"They broke her," I whisper, but no one hears me.

"Both witches were dragged here by the baying mob!" Mr Patterson is almost in a frenzy, enthused by his own story. He gestures up to the old, gnarled tree behind him.

"While hanging was more common in England than Scotland, here witches were more likely to be burned, the Juniper residents decided to use this very tree to carry out their vigilante sentence."

Suddenly I come apart. The mask slips away and I'm making a hoarse, bellowing sound. I hold my sides and rock, finding the muddy ground beneath me in order to feel some stability. I can feel everyone's heads shooting around to look. I keep my eyes tightly shut. I don't want to see the tree, don't want to look at it.

Mr Patterson and Miss Murphy are on either side of me and Audrey is loudly asking if I am all right.

I'm sure I don't look all right.

"Now, stop this silliness," Miss Murphy says, thrusting a water bottle under my nose. "It's just a story."

Just a story. "But it was real!" I gasp.

"Yes, but a very long time ago," Mr Patterson says, trying to reassure me and failing.

Miss Murphy leaves us to go and gather the other children. She mutters something to Mr Patterson that I cannot hear over the blood pounding in my ears.

"Now, let's walk along to the bridge and we can move onto that Robert Burns poem I asked you to read for homework."

"Can I stay with Addie, Miss?" Audrey asks.

"No," Miss Murphy says firmly. "Leave her to calm down, she'll join us when she's finished."

They begin to leave.

"No need to be so upset," Mr Patterson says in a jolly tone as I desperately try to control my breathing. "It was very sad, but like I said… a very long time ago."

"They killed them because they were different."

"Well, yes. Mary was an imbecile and Jean was—"

"I hate that word."

"Well, nowadays we would say she had special needs—"

"Like me. She was like me."

His face drains of colour. It's almost funny. He starts to stammer in embarrassment while I try to put my invisible mask back on. I force myself to make eye contact with him, something I hate, something that feels unnatural and painful sometimes.

"I am not an imbecile."

"No, of course not," he bleats.

Maggie, Jean and Mary. Tricked and cornered, lied to and lied about. I feel despair for all three of them, so much that I can't breathe.

I stagger to a standing position and take a big swig of lukewarm water. I am gasping for breath after swallowing. I hand him the bottle and begin to slowly move up to re-join the group. I ignore the tree. I don't look at it.

I stare ahead, pushing past branches that look like skeletal hands reaching out, begging for help.

Chapter Eight

"Addie has a very overactive imagination."

I'm sitting with Mum and Dad in the Primary Six classroom. Miss Murphy and Mr Patterson are both here, too. The trip ended and Miss Murphy said that she'd called them in for a meeting to discuss what happened.

"I am well aware of that, Mr Darrow," Miss Murphy says to Dad, with a big warm smile. I've never seen her smile like this before. "We just wanted to make sure that we can find ways to stop this from happening again."

She beams at me and I realise that it might be the very first time I've seen such an expression directed at me. From her.

"You're not in any trouble, Adeline," she adds, still smiling.

"No," Mum chimes in. "Addie, you're not in trouble at all. Did you just get overwhelmed? Overstimulated?"

I nod.

"It's a very grisly story," Mr Patterson says, looking apologetic. "But the kids usually love that!"

"The other children were enjoying the experience,"

Miss Murphy tells my parents gently. "Adeline just got far too emotional."

I can feel Mum and Dad exchanging a look over the top of my head.

"Addie feels things quite deeply," Mum admits after a small pause. "It's part of her being autistic."

Miss Murphy's smile flickers. Mum and Dad don't see it.

"And she's been really intrigued by this term's project," Dad says. "You know, all she talks about at home is witchcraft now. I think today was just a bit much."

"Well, I'm really glad you're interested," Mr Patterson says cheerfully. "It is fascinating."

"It's just…" I speak for the first time. "They were real people. And no one seems to care."

None of the adults say anything.

"History can be a difficult subject if you get too emotionally attached," Mr Patterson says, strangely cheerful. "Wars, famine. Witch trials. You have to detach yourself from it all."

"She's trying," Dad says in response. "And we don't really want Addie to lose her compassion."

"Yes, well," Mr Patterson splays his hands out and gestures at me. "It's quite refreshing, I know most children with autism don't have a lot of empathy so it's good to see."

Mum makes a rattling sound in her throat. Dad reaches over and presses down on her thigh.

"I'm autistic," I correct him, almost automatically. "It's something you are, not something you have. And that's a common misunderstanding. Autistic people are actually very…"

"Empathetic," Mum assists.

"Yeah."

Mr Patterson goes a little red.

"How many autistic people do you know, Mr Patterson?" I ask, genuinely curious.

"Oh, well, I," he tugs at his collar. "Well, none, I suppose."

"Except me."

"Yes," he nods slowly, smiling sheepishly. "Except you. Addie."

"Autism isn't a personality difference," Mum says firmly. "It's not a matter of Addie being a little more sensitive or a little more emotional. She is dealing with a different neurological reality. A cognitive difference. She needs structure, support and understanding."

There is a small pause before Mum adds, "We want Addie to have a better childhood than our other daughter had."

Miss Murphy arches an eyebrow at the mention of Keedie and stares Mum down. Mum stares back.

"I just worry that the classroom is sometimes a little much for Adeline," Miss Murphy finally says. "I have a lot of children to teach, they all deserve equal attention, so I sometimes wonder if Adeline would be better off somewhere where she can get real one to one care and attention."

I'm puzzled by this. She hardly ever addresses me in lessons, unless it's to tell me to put my hand down or improve my handwriting. She's talking to Mum and Dad as if she has to sit with me all day, every day. In fact, she spends most of her time with Emily. Especially in English and spelling.

"No," Mum says firmly. "Addie needs normality. She's an independent worker, very gifted, if she just gets the right direction. All her previous teachers have said so. They all loved her."

They go back to staring each other down.

I pick up my bag and turn to Mum, eyes lowered. "Can we go home now?"

Mum smiles, polite but tired. "We'll chat about this at home with Addie. Is there anything else we need to discuss?"

"No," Miss Murphy stands. "We just wanted you to

know what happened and let Adeline know that she's got support here."

Mum and Dad say thank you and turn to go. As their backs are turned, Miss Murphy's broad smile vanishes. She casts a glance at me, her eyes hard and cold. Then looks away.

I follow Mum and Dad out. I think Miss Murphy wears a mask, too.

A different kind of mask.

*

"She's a vicious cow."

"Keedie!"

We are all sitting around the kitchen table. It's rare, usually one of my parents is working. We are eating takeaway that has been put on nice plates. Nina is eating her chicken noodles and not speaking. Keedie is furious. I try and imagine what a vicious cow would look like. It's difficult. Cows are not vicious, at least the Juniper ones aren't. They're very nosy, actually. But quite easy to talk to.

But it doesn't seem a good time to point that out, Keedie isn't finished.

"She couldn't have told the guest speaker not to throw around antiquated terms?" Keedie takes an angry bite out of a prawn cracker. "She couldn't have asked him to dial down the nasty details?"

"Most of the children like the gory details," Dad points out. "It's just a mistake, it's no one's fault, Keedie."

"Addie," Mum speaks gently, putting some more rice in front of me. "You know if anyone says anything at school that upsets you, you have to tell a grown-up? Were people mean to you today? Is that why you were upset?"

"No," I pick up my spoon. "I just felt what the witches were feeling."

"It's wonderful that you're so concerned, darling," Mum says steadily. "You can channel that into your campaigning. But when you're overwhelmed or overstimulated, you need to tell an adult."

I know she's right. And if it had been Mrs Hazel or Miss Elspeth, some of my former teachers, I would have. They always listened and found time for me.

But Miss Murphy is different.

"Miss Murphy might not understand everything about you right away," Mum says firmly. "She's from a different generation. And the poor woman must be run ragged with her mother being so ill and the husband gone. She might not have all the patience in the world, but she's hardly the monster you want to make her, Keeds."

"Keedie only sees in black and white," Nina says softly.

"Not true, I can see all the hideous beige things you wear."

"Shut up."

"Girls!" Mum snaps at my sisters. "Enough."

"Miss Murphy's probably a bit scarred from her time with Keedie," Dad says teasingly.

"I hope so," Keedie replies heartily. "She was the worst. She always played favourites with the other kids, so I'd let her have it every now and then."

"Oh, Keedie," Mum exhales wearily. "No wonder she's wary of Addie."

"She doesn't get to punish Addie because of me," Keedie points out. "Anyway, she's not got a clue about how to teach kids with different support needs."

"Well, few people do and teachers have to do so much nowadays," Mum says reasonably.

"You know," Dad looks over at me, "Grandpa had trouble at school."

"He told me he used to get the belt!" I exclaim.

"He did! He had trouble concentrating so the teacher would whack his hand with a belt."

"Better than doing lines, he said," I say.

"It probably was."

"Well, Miss Murphy would never belt any of us," I say cheerily. "So it's not that bad."

For a while, the only sound in the kitchen is the scraping of cutlery against crockery.

"How's Jenna these days, Addie?" Dad asks. "You don't mention her as much. Still wanting to be a hairdresser?"

"I don't know."

They exchange another one of their looks. More scraping. More silence.

"How's uni?" Mum finally asks Keedie.

Keedie makes a face. "Fine. Boring."

"Is it hard?" Dad smiles encouragingly.

"Work is good," Keedie says, taking some spring rolls. "People are hard."

I want Keedie to look at me but she doesn't. She's the first in our family to go to university. When she got her unconditional offer, Mum and Dad both cried.

She didn't seem that happy about it though.

"So many doors are going to open for you now, Keeds," says Dad excitedly. "So many opportunities."

"Yeah," Nina says quietly. "You won't have to be an assistant manager at a local supermarket."

There is a stunned silence.

"That was a horrible thing to say, Nina," I whisper.

"You can leave this table right now!" Mum bellows, all of her stress and exhaustion boiling over.

Nina throws her cutlery down and storms out of the kitchen, slamming the door behind her. Mum leaps to her feet and starts clearing the table, even though we're still eating. Keedie just manages to rescue a piece of chicken from her plate before it is snatched away.

"Neurotypical people," Keedie sighs, finally looking at me with a grin. "So lacking in empathy. It's so very sad."

I snort. Juice almost comes out of my nose. Dad laughs, reluctantly.

I sit with Dad in the living room while Mum and Nina have a screaming match upstairs. Keedie sits next to me. The three of us rest against the back of the sofa, saying not one word. I watch Dad. He looks sad. Tired.

I get onto my knees and scurry across the carpet to the CD player. Dad's favourite album is the second in a teetering pile of discs, quite worn with a few scratches. I slip it into the player.

Sunshine on Leith plays comfortingly, drowning out the shouting from upstairs. I sit back on the sofa between Dad and Keedie. The three of us sway imperceptibly to the song. Dad starts to hum along.

Dad reaches over to squeeze my hand once. Firmly and quickly. I do the same to Keedie.

Mum and Nina carry on upstairs, their voices faint, using words as a weapon. Cutting each other down with the power of speech. When I'm angry or upset, the words rarely come - I find speaking suddenly very challenging. It's not like that for Mum or Nina.

Dad, Keedie and I sit contentedly with the music washing over us. Not needing to communicate a thing.

*

"What happened to you on the school trip?"

Audrey and I are sitting by the bike sheds having lunch. I've given her my crisps and she's given me her biscuit.

"I was starting to shut down," I say plainly. "The story Mr Patterson was telling was making me… it was hard to listen to. So I needed to stim, but I knew I couldn't, so then I got really panicky."

Audrey nods but I know she doesn't fully grasp it yet. I think it must be hard for neurotypical people to imagine a completely different way of thinking and feeling. A heightened one where everything is louder, brighter. Better. Worse.

"I just felt a bit desperate," I say, pulling the chocolate biscuit apart so I can eat the different sections one by one.

"Are you still campaigning for that memorial?"

"Yep." I lay the biscuit pieces in my lap. "They've turned me down but I'm going to keep trying. Keedie says we should make flyers to hand out."

"Can I help?"

I look up, surprised. "Yes! That would be great."

"I'm good at drawing. We can make flyers now and use the copier in the library."

I nod, eagerly. In our rush to get to Mr Allison, I just scoff the entire biscuit whole.

*

"Hello, Addie!"

I look up from our table at the library. It's Miss Latimer, the drama teacher.

"I'm looking forward to seeing you after half-term for drama," she says merrily, glancing at Audrey who is furiously scribbling on a colourful flyer.

"Me, too," I say truthfully, smiling up at her. She's the youngest looking teacher, but I don't think she is the youngest. If that makes sense.

"Jacobites next term," she says beaming. "You know, I remember when Keedie was in my class and we were doing Jacobites. She climbed up onto a bench and acted out the entire battle of Killiecrankie by herself! Finished with a very impressive soldier's leap."

I giggle. Keedie loves history and makes me love it too. She recounts stories of famous battles and will dance around the room, playing all of the characters. Her Marie-Antoinette is one of my favourites. Followed closely by Robert the Bruce.

"What are you girls doing?"

"We're campaigning," Audrey answers, lifting up her drawing.

"Oh, wow. What for?"

"Addie wants the Juniper assembly members to set up a memorial for all of the witches that were killed here in the past."

Miss Latimer looks startled for a moment and then her face breaks into an enormous smile. "I think that's absolutely wonderful!"

"Really?" I think Miss Latimer is the most amazing teacher, and I really want her to like my idea. I don't want her to think it's stupid, like Miss Murphy did.

"That's a fantastic idea, Addie," she assures me. "I'm actually really proud of you. It's important to fight for what's right."

Keedie always says 'thank goodness for drama teachers'. I see why.

Miss Latimer says goodbye and heads to lunch and I feel an extra burst of determination.

"She's right," Audrey says carefully, changing one colourful pencil for another. "This is the right thing to do."

I nod.

"Is Keedie your other sister?"

"Yes. She's Nina's twin. But they're not identical. Not in any way. And she's autistic, like me."

"So... why isn't Nina autistic?"

I shrug. "Don't know. You're born autistic and Nina just wasn't born that way."

"Oh."

"Keedie had a hard time growing up though," I say, pulling the flyer towards me for examination. "She had this friend when she was just a bit older than me. Bonnie.

They met when Keedie was seeing an occupational therapist after her diagnosis. Bonnie would get overstimulated and her shutdowns sometimes got really bad."

I stroke a finger over the witch Audrey has drawn on the paper.

"And Bonnie only had her mum, who was not very well, so they struggled to get help sometimes. And then one day she got taken away."

I can feel Audrey's eyes on me. "Taken away?"

"To a place for kids with mental health issues. She was sectioned. Autism isn't a mental illness, but they didn't care."

"What happened?"

"Well, Bonnie's meltdowns must have scared all of the neurotypical people. She would never hurt anyone! I met her, she would never. She might hurt herself if she was frightened. But never other people. But they locked her up anyway."

"I didn't know they could do that."

"She was allowed out for walks and visits. But when she turned eighteen…"

I pause. Audrey has drawn the old, gnarled tree. The hanging tree. She's a talented artist, it looks exactly like the real thing.

"They moved her to a new facility. Meaner people. And no hatch on the door. No windows. Just four walls."

I feel a tightness in my chest. A sharp, aching pain.

"Can't her mum take her home? Make them let her out?"

"When you're sectioned," I try to remember exactly how Mum explained it to me, "the state sort of owns you. They decide what to do with you. Not your family. And not you."

"But that's not fair!"

"I know."

Keedie had described her last visit with Bonnie, before she was moved to the adult facility. The hatch in the door had been small, the size of a paperback. It had been wrenched open and Bonnie's pale, trembling hands appeared. Reaching out.

Keedie said they were cold as she held onto them.

"It's like the witches," I say, pushing the flyer back towards Audrey. "They've made up their minds about Bonnie. And, in a way, people have made up their minds about me and Keedie. What we are."

Audrey glance down at her drawing, looking slightly withdrawn. "That's why you got so upset on the trip."

"I know if I get too overstimulated in public, if no one is there to explain it, people might think I'm dangerous.

That I'm trying to hurt people."

"But you're not!"

"I know. But lots of people still don't understand."

We sit in silence for a moment.

"This memorial's really important to me, Audrey,"
I say roughly. "It's hard to explain why. Jean, Mary…
those women. They didn't sound dangerous at all to me,
they sounded scared. Different and scared."

She nods. I feel exhausted. It takes an unbelievable
amount of energy to communicate like this, to emote
like this, and I have a headache from it all.

"We should get Mr Allison to make copies of this and
then hand them out after school," Audrey says decidedly,
gathering her things.

I nod. But my stinging head is still with Keedie.
And Bonnie.

Chapter Nine

"What the hell are you doing?"

Audrey and I are handing out flyers just outside of Juniper's only bookshop, Dogood Books. It should be perfectly obvious to Nina, who barks the question at us from the driver's seat of Mum's car, what we are doing.

"You shouldn't be driving that," I tell my sister defiantly. "You haven't got your full licence."

"Addie, you can't just run off gallivanting after school." She gets out of the car and slams the door. "I was really worried, you were supposed to be home an hour ago."

"We're campaigning," I tell her and Audrey hands her a flyer. "Not gallivanting. We've been stationed here for half an hour."

She glances at the flyer briefly before returning her glare to me. "Get in the car."

"We haven't finished yet," I say stiffly. "Cleo's taken a bunch to put in her shop, but we still have more to hand out."

Cleo runs Dogood Books and was very enthusiastic about the idea. Good booksellers, like good teachers, are saviours.

"Are you Audrey?" Nina addresses my new friend, putting on her grown-up face and voice. "I'm sure your parents are worried about you being out here on your own as well."

"Audrey's from London, Nina," I inform her wearily. "They're not scared of anything in Juniper."

Audrey chuckles.

"Both of you, in the car. Now."

We exchange a look and finally relent.

"She's not as nice as she seems in her videos," Audrey whispers to me.

We get into the back of the car and Nina climbs into the front.

"What's your address?" she asks Audrey, looking at us through the rear-view mirror.

"I'm on Woodburn street."

"Ok, good."

Nina drives off. "So what did you learn today?" she asks, still playing at being a grown-up.

"That Keedie used to re-enact Jacobite battles in drama lessons."

"Oh, God," Nina whispers under her breath. "Good to know that years after leaving that primary school, Keedie's legacy still lives on."

"Yeah," I say cheerfully, deliberately ignoring her sarcasm.

"I found out that the government can lock people like Addie up if they want to."

The car stalls suddenly. "What did you say?"

"I told her about Bonnie, Nina."

"Oh, Addie," Nina turns the wheel, heading into Audrey's street. "You shouldn't tell people... it's complicated, Audrey. And no one is going to lock Addie away."

"Yeah, as long as I'm good," I mutter.

Nina glances at me in the mirror but says nothing more.

*

I eat my parsnip soup and keep an eye on the kitchen window for Keedic. I have a flyer waiting on the table to show her. Nina is eating silently and Mum has gone up to bed after a long shift.

"Audrey is a really good cartoonist," Dad says, studying the flyer. "I'm impressed."

"Yeah, she's going to help me campaign," I tell him, eating another mouthful of soup.

"That's excellent. Maybe on Sunday you can leave some at the kirk."

"Because the church is going to be enthusiastic about pardoning witches?" Nina says dryly.

The kitchen window slides open before anyone can respond. Keedie's golden head ducks inside and her tall body follows.

If I had a tail, it would wag.

"Evening, troops."

She falls into her seat and beams briefly at me before getting herself some soup.

She's smiling and acting cheerful, but her eyes look a little tired and her colour a little dulled. I can't make sense of it.

"Keedie, look at my flyer!" I rush to hand it to her.

"Let her eat, Addie," Nina admonishes quietly.

Keedie ignores her and grabs the drawing. "Well. Isn't this a bit of fantastic? Addie, did you draw this?"

"No, Audrey did," I tell her. "She's on the team."

"Amazing."

"I told her why it matters. And I told her about Bonnie."

Keedie's eyes shoot up to meet mine, her smile gone. "What?"

I glance from Keedie to Nina. She's watching Keedie intently. My voice shakes a little as I explain. "I told her what they did to Bonnie."

"She thinks it's similar, Keedie," Nina says softly. "The witches… she thinks it's the same."

Keedie slowly passes the flyer back, laying it gently on the table. "It is the same."

I exhale heavily. I knew it was the same. I knew Keedie would understand.

"Bonnie's situation is under control," Dad says calmly. "No one has forgotten her; your Mum is keeping tabs on the whole thing."

"Yeah," Keedie says flatly, getting up. "But she's still stuck in that awful place."

She leaves the room. I glance down at the flyer and then take off after her, ignoring Dad and Nina's calls for me to finish dinner.

I find her in the street, in front of our house. Sitting on the kerb under a streetlight. Looking up at the sparks in the darkness, each one a bright pinprick in the clear Scottish sky.

"They don't get it, Addie."

I slowly sit down beside her. "Get what?"

"What it's like. To have to hide every day. To pretend."

"I know," I press my arm against hers. "If the witches didn't pretend well enough, they were caught out. And punished."

"You know why Bonnie's gone away, don't you, Addie?"

"Because she couldn't mask anymore."

"Yes. And those…" she stops herself before she says a bad word. "Those people didn't want to help her."

"That's why this is important to me, Keedie," I say quietly, almost too quietly. "They all think it's just a story. But it was real. And it happened here."

"I know."

"I try," I blink rapidly, "I try really hard to hide. But sometimes I don't want to. I don't want to, Keedie."

"I know," she says soothingly. "I know, Addie. And you shouldn't have to. You should feel safe to be yourself all the time. We shouldn't have to mask."

"But I get scared," I look down at my hands, they're humming with invisible sparks. Overstimulated. Desperate to grab hold of something. "I don't want to… to end up—"

"Listen," she's not looking into my eyes and yet I feel her full attention on me. "I will never let that happen. They'd have to get through me, Addie, and they never will. That will never happen."

I once had a meltdown in the supermarket. I don't remember much of it, just lying on the cold floor by one of the freezers, trying to breathe. Keedie stood over me, admonishing anyone that tried to come near me.

She had seemed so grown up and mature then, all of those years ago. But she had only been my age. The age I am now.

"You'll always be here, Keedie."

It isn't a question. She smiles at me.

"You know, my uni professors love to tell us all to 'think outside of the box'," she says casually.

I smile. "But you're not inside the box."

Her eyes dance. "Exactly."

"We never have been."

And maybe never will be. Whatever goes on inside that box with other people, I don't understand it. I always feel like everyone else has been sent pages and pages of instructions, tips and tricks to life and how to move smoothly.

I'm always a few steps behind. I can read a book in a day, memorise anything, feel things so strongly. But the doublespeak and the secret looks. I'm not sure I'll ever decipher them.

"Someone made a response video to Nina's," I hear myself say it, not realising that it has been on my mind. "It was a woman shouting about how I'm not a proper autistic."

Keedie exhales. "I wish you would have left it alone."

"Why was she so angry?"

"Because," Keedie rubs her face with both of her hands, "there are so many different ways to be autistic, Addie. And some people don't understand that."

We sit in silence for moment.

"Besides," Keedie finally says, "you shouldn't listen to people that shout and say nasty things on the internet. They're the lowest of the low. You should care about what you think."

"And you!"

She smirks and looks down at her feet. "Sure, me too."

I run my fingertips along the rough texture of the pavement.

"You know, Addie," Keedie lowers her voice and glances back at the house, "Nina never wanted any of those horrible things to happen. She didn't mean any harm."

I grin. Keedie hardly ever stands up for Nina. "I know that."

Chapter Ten

The school is closed today for an inset day, something Mum says teachers need for additional development, whatever that means. Dad has already gone to the supermarket to start his shift and Mum is putting her coat on and packing up her handbag.

"Now, Addie," she looks at me sternly as she zips up her enormous, padded coat. "Nina will be here all day looking after you so ask her if you need anything. Don't go outside without her and don't answer the phone."

I hate answering the phone anyway so I don't argue that point. Nina is scrolling through her phone next to me, seemingly not listening.

"Nina," Mum's tone tells us both that she is having, as Dad says, a sense of humour failure. "No locking yourself away and filming today, all right? Stay with Addie, stay downstairs."

Nina grunts and continues to scroll. Mum looks as if she is going to say something for a moment but she just shakes her head, pats me on the hand and then leaves for work.

A few moments after the front door closes, Nina slides out of her chair. Still glued to her phone.

"I'm filming all of today," she says matter-of-factly. "Knock on my door at one and I'll make you lunch."

She disappears upstairs.

I'm about to do the same when I notice something. On the kitchen counter, by the door, is a stack of papers that Keedie put down on Friday. Her student ID card is poking out from underneath them.

I snatch it up, panicked. Keedie brought us all on a tour of the university a few months ago and the student giving the tour kept mentioning how important the ID card was, and advising Keedie to never lose it.

I dig through the kitchen drawer, knowing Dad throws his change in here. There are tons of pennies, so I gather together enough for a return ticket on the bus. I slip them all into my jean pocket and put the ID card in as well.

As I reach the front door, I glance up the stairs. I know if I tell Nina she'll say no. I also know that the bus takes twenty minutes to get into Edinburgh, so I can get there and back in ninety minutes.

And Nina never has to find out.

The door closes softly behind me, my mind made up.

I sprint to the one and only Juniper bus stop and catch

my breath while I wait. It's quite exciting; like being on a mission. I squeeze Keedie's ID pass in my pocket as the bus rounds the corner.

The bus driver doesn't seem overly impressed with my many coins but he finally gives me a return ticket. I sit by the window and watch Juniper disappear as we head into Edinburgh, and I cannot help fidgeting. I'm worried for Keedie, worried that she's in trouble or being told off.

I've always had a good memory. Once I've been to a place, I can always picture it in my mind and retrace my steps. I can remember how to get to the university because we all went there with Keedie. Once, on holiday in a caravan park, I got bored during the kid's camp activities and wandered off. I was able to walk all the way back to our caravan, where a terrified Mum and Dad eventually found me after the day camp noticed I had gone missing.

They perhaps don't understand that my brain can turn into a map.

The bus drives along Princes Street and I look up at the castle. It overlooks what used to be the loch. The one Miss Murphy says the witches were taken to. I almost miss my stop as I try to imagine what those scenes must have looked like.

I run up the mound, through the Royal Mile, beyond the statue with the golden toe, beyond Greyfriars Bobby and onwards to the building I remember.

Once I'm inside the building, my confidence wavers a little. The ceilings seem so high, everyone around me so grown-up and busy. I suddenly realise that I don't know which lecture she has today, what hall she will be in.

I poke my head into what looks like an office, one like the admin office at our school. A woman with a big mug of tea looks up and is comically startled by the sight of me.

"Are you… are you lost?"

"Um, sort of," I invite myself into the office and stand in front of her desk. "I need to find my sister, Keedie Darrow. She's a student here."

"Right," the woman puts her mug down, looking very nervous. "And is it an emergency?"

I think about how insistent that tour guide was about not losing the pass. "Yes."

"Okay, let me just check," she turns to her computer, still looking a little dazed. "Darrow?"

"Yes."

"And it's an emergency?"

"Yes."

"All right."

She types for a little while I hop from one leg to the other, impatient.

Finally, she grabs a piece of scrap paper and scribbles a lecture hall location onto it and hands it over. I grab it and start to run out of the office before remembering my manners.

I poke my head back in. "Thank you!"

I have to ask people for help to find the classroom. The university building is so enormous, so grand, and everyone seems to know exactly where they're going, except me. Someone finally points me in the right direction, and I have to get a lift up two floors.

When I eventually reach the right door, I feel suddenly afraid. I can see through the glass panel that the door is at the back of a large lecture theatre, with a lecturer down at the front in the middle of a class.

There are big words up on the projector. There are many students scattered throughout the hall.

I push open the door. The lecturer stops. He glances up at me, squinting. People's heads turn.

And I spot her.

While all the other students are sitting in little groups, Keedie sits alone near the front. She's wearing a dark denim dress and knee length black boots, as well as her sunglasses. They're special shades with prescriptions in them; she needs them to see but also to shield out the fluorescent lighting.

Those lights feel piercing as I stand in the room. I wince. It's too bright; even with her glasses on, this must be hellish for Keedie. The temperature is horrid, not pleasant at all. I can see within seconds how uncomfortable Keedie is, and how relaxed everyone else seems.

She glances back and, while I cannot read her expression with the glasses on, she is obviously stunned to see me.

"Can I help?" the lecturer calls out, looking up at me in confusion and curiosity.

"It's my sister," Keedie says quickly, getting out of her seat and running up the aisle of the lecture theatre. She steers me out of the room while some of the students snicker. She shuts the door on their titters and grabs my shoulders.

"What's wrong, is it Nina?"

"No." I dig in my pocket and pull out the student ID pass, triumphantly. "Here!"

She doesn't say anything for a moment, taking it from my outstretched hand and staring at it as if she has never seen it before.

"Addie… did you come all the way here to give this back?"

"Yes."

She doesn't seem pleased or relieved and I suddenly get a sick feeling. Have I misjudged? Made a mistake?

"Is," she glances around the empty corridor we are in, "is Nina here?"

"No, I slipped away."

"Addie, you shouldn't have."

Keedie suddenly grimaces as if she's in incredible pain. She holds her sides and turns her back on me. I watch her try to steady her breathing, one hand pressed against the wall, and I feel a shiver of fear run down my back.

"Keedie, what's wrong?"

She isn't turning around. She won't look at me.

"I… I can't." She tries to speak but stops.

Something is badly wrong. I wonder if the surprise of seeing me has thrown her. Neither of us like surprises. Maybe it was the lights in the classroom? I was only in there for a few seconds, and it made me feel rubbish.

I've seen Keedie overstimulated before, but I've never seen her struggle with speech.

"Keedie, are you okay? I'm sorry, I thought it was really important. How do you cope with this place anyway? It's awful and it's swampy and too bright and too loud and too busy."

She closes her eyes, I can just make them out behind the shades. She digs out her mobile phone with violently shaking hands and sighs when she sees a long list of notifications.

I can see all of the missed calls on the phone screen.

She wraps an arm and my shoulder and starts walking us out of the building. She dials Nina's number while doing so.

"Hi," she says shakily when Nina answers. "She's here, I've got her—"

Though I cannot make out what she's saying, I can hear Nina speaking rapidly on the other end of the phone.

Then she hangs up.

"Is Nina coming to get us or are we getting the bus?"

Keedie glances at me and shakes her head. I can see it's still difficult for her to speak as she simply says, "Mum."

I can feel all of the colour draining from my face.

*

"You've been impossible lately but this is a new low."

Nina scowls at Mum's words, the four of us in the car heading back to Juniper.

"I called you, didn't I?" Nina responds angrily. "The minute I noticed she was gone."

"You should have been with her the entire time!" bellows Mum. She's not a large woman but she can reach an incredible volume of noise. "You heard my instructions and you deliberately disobeyed me. And she could have been picked up by anyone! Anything could have happened."

I frown from the backseat. Grown-ups always do this. They tell you the world is dangerous, that strangers are bad, but they never tell you why. They say to be afraid but never give you a reason.

"I was bad, Mum," I say nervously. "I knew it was wrong. I thought I would get back without Nina noticing."

"Which further proves my point," Mum says, hitting the steering wheel in frustration. "You were meant to be watched full-time."

"Can we take the yelling down to a five?" asks Keedie, her head pressed against the car window and her brow furrowed. "It's loud in this car."

"Addie, when an adult tells you not to do something, you don't do it. And if they tell you to do something, you do it. Okay? You knew you weren't to go out and you did it anyway." She glares from me to Nina. "You both know better."

I don't say anything. Surely adults can't know best all of the time. I don't think Miss Murphy does.

"She was scared I was going to get into trouble without my ID pass," Keedie says slowly. "She misunderstood, she made a mistake. Leave off her now."

"Addie, you can't keep running around after Keedie all of the time," Mum says, her voice starting to calm down. "Especially if it means breaking the rules."

I look out at the city as it flashes by. "I was afraid she was going to be in trouble."

Mum exhales. "I know. But you have to look at the whole picture. Nina found out you were gone, called me and here we are. You should have told Nina about the pass. You should have spoken to a grown-up. You made some bad decisions today, kid. And I know your heart was in the right place but that doesn't always matter if something bad happens."

"Nothing bad happened," I say stonily. I look across at Keedie. She isn't looking back, she's staring out of the window and giving me nothing.

"Why are you like this right now?" I ask desperately. "Why are you different?"

She laughs but it's not a nice laugh. "I'm always different."

"Not like this," I insist. "This is new. You're not the same. You could barely speak earlier!"

Nina turns around as I say this. She fixes Keedie with a look of concern. "What?"

"Nothing," Keedie growls.

"She was struggling to talk!" I say indignantly. "She was! That university is horrid, none of it is built for people like us."

"Addie, nowhere is built for people like us," Keedie murmurs.

"The library is!" I snap. "Mr Allison makes sure everything is quiet and organised and spread out."

"Is it happening again?" Nina asks Keedie quietly, barely audible over the noise of the car.

"Nina," Mum speaks sharply. "University is hard. Keedie is still adjusting."

"Why won't you tell me what's wrong?" I push, ignoring Mum and addressing Keedie.

"Because nothing is wrong," Keedie says, smiling at me smoothly. I can't see if her eyes are smiling too. "Nothing is wrong, Addie, I'm fine. Don't worry about me."

I sit back in my seat and glare out of the window.

"You're lying."

Chapter Eleven

Audrey and I are almost late to school because we meet a chocolate Labrador on the way. He is wonderfully playful and excitable, happy to see us and to play. I'm desperate for the day when I can have a pet. Animals are almost always preferable to people, although I like Audrey more and more with each day. She has some good jokes and is great at doing impressions of the teachers and people from television. We are laughing as we arrive at the gates. Jenna and Emily are waiting by reception, making sure that we see them whispering and laughing.

"They have so little in their lives," says Audrey and it makes me think. She is right. When I'm with Audrey, we're too busy having fun to be mean to other people.

Audrey links arms with me firmly and we head inside the school, heads held high and barely able to stop our giggles from breaking free. We're putting away our coats when I hear a small and quiet voice say, "Addie?"

I turn to see Jenna, alone without Emily.

"Yes?" Audrey says for me.

"Can I talk to you, Addie?"

"We're talking now," I say, frowning.

"No, in private?"

I don't really see the point but I follow her to the female toilets. Once we are inside, I turn to ask what she wants to talk about but am surprised to find Emily there, stepping out of one of the stalls.

"You think you're so clever," she says sharply, getting right up close to me. "You're not. You're actually well and truly mental. So don't ever think about laughing at Jenna or me again. Got it?"

I feel like I've stepped into one of the terrible films that Nina likes to watch. Emily is speaking like a character on a screen. She and Jenna want so badly to grow up.

"We weren't laughing at you."

"Shut up!"

"Maybe you shouldn't laugh at people," I say sternly. "If you hate it so much, you shouldn't do it to other people. You should have some," I mentally flick open my thesaurus, "empathy."

An unnameable look flickers across Emily's face before she turns it into a sneer. "You don't even know what empathy is. Your damaged brain can't feel it."

Mum always says some people don't deserve a response. So I turn and leave the toilets, refusing to give her a reaction.

I make it to our classroom just in time. Audrey flashes me a look which I think is asking me what happened. I concentrate and give her one that says I will tell her later.

Miss Murphy enters and tells one of the boys to hand out the mathematic workbooks. I feel my spine stiffen. Maths. I can tell Miss Murphy is not feeling patient, and I am terrible at maths. We're doing long multiplication and it takes me ages to work it out.

Sure enough, we are set a page of thirteen problems to solve.

"In absolute silence," Miss Murphy says. "No conferring."

I stare at the numbers in front of me. I feel the panic rising. I start to try and work them out. Miss Murphy showed us exactly how to do the workings, and said we shouldn't do it any other way. But it doesn't work for me. I try it another way. I write the sums out in my own fashion.

It's easier. It works.

I feel torn. It seems right. It feels right. But it doesn't look like anybody else's.

The lesson continues and, for the first time, I solve every problem. I hand in my workbook with everybody else, feeling a sense of relief and accomplishment.

I tell Audrey all about it at the library, while we eat lunch.

"I hate maths," she says, shivering and taking a large bite out of an apple. "My brother says we don't need any of it."

"Is your brother here or in London?"

"He's in Oxford," she replies. "Studying."

"What's London like?"

"Well," she thinks for a moment. "I think you could probably fit a million Junipers in London and still have room."

"No way."

"Yes way."

I marvel at the thought. "Could you see the big clock from your old house?"

"No," she says. "We lived in Tower Hamlets, near Canary Wharf. When I was little, I thought the skyline was New York City. I'm going to move there one day."

"Wow."

I turn the page of my book.

"Is this one about sharks?"

"No," I turn it round so that she can see. "Witches."

"Of course."

I read a little more while she finishes her apple.

"What do you love about sharks so much?"

I light up at the question. "I love everything about them. Their ancestors were here millions of years before the dinosaurs. That's so old, I can't even get my mind around it."

"That is old. But don't they eat people?"

"No," I shake my head adamantly. "They might take a bite out of someone, thinking that they're a seal, but they don't hunt or eat humans."

"I don't know," she giggles. "I think they're horrible."

The light in me dims. I retreat to my book, embarrassed and saddened. Audrey notices and says, "I mean, I think it's cool how much you know about them."

I feel defensive. "They're amazing fish. Really smart."

"I like dolphins."

"Everyone likes dolphins," I say sadly. "I don't see why they're any better than sharks."

"They just seem friendlier," she points out. "Less scary."

I nod absently and go back to my book. I feel a little empty. Flat. I feel that maybe we weren't talking about sharks and dolphins at all.

Chapter Twelve

"I'll meet you in the classroom," I tell Audrey as the warning bell rings. She looks confused but nods. I put my book on witches away and draw the shark book from my bag. I take it up to Mr Allison's desk.

"Finished already? You're getting even quicker," he says cheerily.

"I don't want it anymore," I say quietly.

His smile fades. "Oh. Addie, why?"

I fight the ridiculous urge to well up. "They're silly. No one likes them."

"Addie," he sits on the edge of his desk and gently takes the book from me. "You like them. That's all that matters."

I wipe at my eyes with my sleeve and look around. "Do you have any books on dolphins?"

"Well," he looks surprised. "Yes, we certainly do. But…"

"I'll take one about dolphins, please."

He pauses before going to fetch one for me. I check it out and slide it into my bag next to the witch book. I can feel him watching me as I head back down the corridor for afternoon lessons.

Only Keedie and I are going to the village meeting this evening. Mum begs us to behave as she leaves for work, giving Keedie an especially hard look. Keedie says we will before winking at me. I laugh.

We arrive at the village hall just in time to grab some seats in the middle. Mr Macintosh starts the meeting and a hush falls over the busy room. I wait impatiently for new business to be announced. It seems to go on forever. Old Miriam Jensen is loudly admonishing Mr Macintosh for interrupting her monologue about the importance of litter clearing in the Juniper woods.

"When half the plastic bags in Scotland seem to end up in my front garden, aren't I permitted to become a little ornery?" she barks at him.

Miriam lives in the largest house in the village but it's hidden in the woods. She doesn't always come to village meetings. In fact, we hardly see her out and about at all. Keedie said that she's a bit of a hermit.

A rich hermit, Nina added.

"Miriam, I've promised you I'll look into that."

"Well, a promise from you is like waiting for my husband to come back from the dead. Pointless!"

"I won't be spoken to like this, Miriam!"

"Aye, well, I survived the war, I'm not afraid of you!"

There is a smattering of disapproval but Keedie and I have to bite our hands to contain our snorts. It's fun to see someone stand toe to toe with Mr Macintosh, making him turn purple with irritation and embarrassment.

When he finally opens the floor, I am the first to my feet.

Determined. Driven. Decided. My thesaurus has hundreds of words to describe how resolved I feel.

"Now, young lady," Mr Macintosh cuts me off before I even speak. "We know what you're going to propose, the answer is still no."

"Why?" Keedie demands.

"What are you proposing?"

I glance over at Miriam Jensen, who called out the question.

"I want Juniper to set up a memorial to honour all of the people accused of witchcraft."

I expect the older woman to roll her eyes or say something disdainful. Instead she fixes me with an expression I cannot name.

"Lots of women were hanged here in Juniper," I hear myself telling the reclusive villager. "Without a proper trial. I've been reading about it all in the school library. And some witches were burned, or put in barrels full of nails."

People make sounds of disgust, which sparks anger in me. How can they sit here and be more displeased by my telling of the truth, than by the truth itself?

Miriam returns her attention to Mr Macintosh. "And what are your issues with such an idea?"

Mr Macintosh makes a noise in his throat and begins counting down on his large, sausage-like fingers. "Expense. Time. Commissioning an artist. It's just too much faff."

"I'll raise the money myself!"

Faces turn in their chairs to stare at me. "I'll raise the money," I repeat. "I'll walk dogs, wash cars, clean people's gardens. I'll raise the money for it, Mr Macintosh. I've already started. I've made flyers, lots of them! With my friend Audrey."

"Young lady," another assembly member speaks. "You could wash every car from here to Timbuktu and still not make enough to pay for it. Sculptures and plaques are expensive. They take a lot of money and planning."

"Well, what about the budget?" Keedie asks brashly.

Mr Macintosh almost chokes upon a laugh of pure disbelief. "That budget," he takes in a deep breath, "is meant for seriously important village matters."

"What, like the pig race?" Keedie snaps back.

"Oi!" Mr McBride, another assembly member, is visibly furious at this remark. "Carruthers is a five-time national champion, he brings a lot of people together when he wins a race. He's going to the Highland Show this year!"

"You'd do well to try and respect the traditions of this village, my girl," Mr Macintosh says to Keedie, patting a sweaty Mr McBride on the arm while firmly forcing him to sit back down behind the table. "These time-honoured customs may be humorous to you, but I assure you that they are not funny to the majority of people in Juniper."

"It's not funny, just tragic," Keedie says glibly.

"I think it's a decent idea," Miriam proclaims, stamping her wooden walking stick down on the floor, like a gavel.

"I'll raise all of the money, Mr Macintosh," I say, desperately. "I will! I promise."

"Oh, let the wee pet try!" a lady at the back of the hall says loudly.

"Yeah," another man chimes in. "Where's the harm?"

"The harm," Mr Macintosh says furiously, "is allowing a child with autism to think that we're indulging this ridiculous idea and then letting her be heartbroken when it doesn't happen."

"Autistic."

He stops. "What's that?"

"I'm autistic. I don't have autism, I am autistic."

He looks about ready to argue but decides against it. "Request denied," he says abruptly.

"Please, Mr Macintosh! Please!" I search through my mind, wondering which neurotypical performance I need to try and get right. What do I need to do to communicate to them how important this is? I've given everyone eye contact, I've made sure that my voice goes up and down with lots of expression. I've done everything that they always want from me, what more can I do?

"Please," I look around the whole room. "The last thing these women knew in this world, the last thing they felt was fear. Fear and pain. Looking out at people who didn't understand them, who had accused them of something they weren't!" I feel all of the unfairness of it building up inside of me.

"You have," my voice trembles, "no idea what it is like to be punished for something you cannot control. You can't, or you wouldn't ignore the importance of this."

"There's a well in Edinburgh for them all," Mr Macintosh says, triumphant in what he thinks is a checkmate move. "That should suffice."

"I've seen it," Keedie chimes in. "It doesn't take full responsibility. It doesn't acknowledge the full evil of it all. It almost blames the victims." She meets my gaze and smiles sadly. "We should do better. Here."

"We'll discuss it," Mr McBride volunteers, though he still looks put out about the pig comment.

As the room dissolves into quiet conversation, and the assembly members huddle together, I move over to speak to Miriam Jensen.

"Thank you for speaking up," I say.

She doesn't look up. So I clear my throat and repeat my thanks.

"I heard you," she barks gruffly. "No point in thanking me, they're not going to agree to it."

I glance at Keedie, who is watching the older woman with a bemused expression.

"Well," I pull my sleeves down over my hands. "Thank you anyway."

She makes a grunting sound, but still will not look at me. I don't mind. I feel like that sometimes. Often.

I sit down next to Keedie. She briefly touches my wrist in support.

"Young lady," Mr Macintosh returns his attention to the room. People's conversation dies down as we await the verdict.

It's yet another refusal.

Yet for some reason, the rejection doesn't hurt as much this time. I know I'm going to keep trying. I know I can keep trying, even when they tell me I can't.

I will decide when to give up.

Chapter Thirteen

"Who are you then?"

Audrey's mum leans against the doorframe and looks down at me with a puzzled expression.

My mouth goes dry and my hands start to fizz, urging me to stim. I don't know why simple things like this make me nervous and afraid but they do. It took a lot to knock on the door.

"Is Audrey free to come and play?" I manage to croak the question.

"Pardon?"

"Is," I'm starting to feel a bit panicky. I don't like meeting new people without someone with me to help, I'm scared of saying the wrong thing. "Is Audrey in?"

"Oh," her face brightens a little. "Are you Addie?"

"Yes."

"Come in, she's just on the phone to her brother but she'll be ready to head out in a bit."

I would much rather wait outside in the front garden but I know that will seem rude so I head inside. The house is like ours but not fully furnished yet, with boxes still piled up around the stairs. I can hear Audrey's clear and confident voice coming from the back of the house, the kitchen, and so I hover in the hall.

"Aren't you a funny little thing, you can come all the way in."

Audrey's mum laughs as she says it. She says 'fing' instead of "thing".

"Addie!"

We both turn to see Audrey come striding down the hall. She's wearing a hoodie with the hood up and has a piece of toast in one hand and a phone in the other. She thrusts the phone into her mum's hands and starts putting her shoes on.

"What time will you be back?" Audrey's mum asks, as she returns the phone to its place on the wall.

"Dunno," Audrey replies as we head out the front door. "Bye."

We head off for the woods. Audrey says she has something to show me.

"We'll go the long way around so you don't have to see that horrible tree," she tells me as we reach the pathway into the trees.

I'm surprised by her consideration. People don't normally think about how to make things less difficult for me.

"Where are we going?" I ask as we move through the

woods, crossing the river and heading deeper into the tall trees.

"You'll see!"

I hate surprises. I like to be able to predict things and know exactly what's going to happen. At Christmas, Dad and Keedie help me as much as possible by mapping out the days and telling me how to prepare for everything.

Otherwise I get overwhelmed.

Even though Audrey is leading us through the woods in order to avoid the Witch Tree, I can still feel its presence. Its ugly, snarling branches and the echoes of cries. Nina said that they're in my head and that I'm imagining them, but so what if I am? They were real. They're in my head now only because they were once real and happening.

My autism is a part of my brain, it doesn't mean it isn't real.

"It's just up this way," Audrey says as we take a divergent path and head into a darker part of the forest.

I like Audrey and trust her so I follow her. Mum says I can be too trusting, that I was too sensitive as a young child and that's why I had trouble making friends. I sometimes didn't know when people were being mean. I thought if they said we were friends, then the meanness was deserved.

But I know Audrey isn't like that. I think about what she said about sharks and a stab of hurt pulses in me. I push it down.

"How are you finding Juniper?" I ask her as we trudge along.

"It's fine," she says, after thinking for a moment. "It's so quiet. Back in London, there were always noises at night. Cars, sirens, people coming home late. Here, there's nothing."

"Mr Moon sometimes gets drunk and sings on our street corner at night," I offer up. I feel protective of Juniper, and don't want Audrey to miss London so much that her parents take her back.

"I miss my old friends sometimes."

I glance at her. I wonder what it's like to have lots of friends. I feel I can only manage one at a time.

"Are you named after a film star?" I ask her.

Nina has lots of framed posters of old Hollywood film stars on her bedroom walls. One is blonde with big red lips and a white dress, another has dark eyes and unnaturally long lashes.

But her favourite is called Audrey. She wears a black dress and sunglasses.

"No, I was named after a man-eating plant," Audrey responds.

I stop in shock. "A what?"

"It's from a film," she assures me, jovially. "An old eighties film that my dad loves."

"With a man-eating plant called Audrey?"

"Yup. My dad and my brother have a film club every Friday night and now I've joined, too. It's either old black and white films or really wacky musicals."

Her smile falters for a moment and she adds, "Well, we did. But Daniel's at Oxford now so it's just me and Dad."

I feel really sorry for her but don't know how to say so. I'd hate for Keedie to move away.

I usually get attached to subjects, and I instantly want to know everything. Like the sharks, like the witches. It's not often I want to know all about people.

But I want to know all about Audrey.

"Our new house is much bigger than our one in London," Audrey volunteers excitedly. "My bedroom is the size of our old living room."

"Yeah, I think there's more space up here."

"Way more!" she says enthusiastically. "Only thing is, the people all kind of look the same here."

I know what she means. When I watch London on the news, all the people look very different. It's like a big coral reef with all different kinds of fish.

Juniper feels more like a goldfish bowl.

"Daniel, my brother… he used to sneak up to this roof garden in Canary Wharf. It was on top of these posh flats and, after lots of begging, he took me up to see it."

"How high up were you?"

Audrey throws her hands up at the sky. "Higher than all of these trees."

I stare. "No way."

"Yes way. Much higher. As high as a crane." She smiles, almost sadly. "And we could see the whole city. All of the skyscrapers and the flats and houses. We could see which ones had lights on. People in their sitting rooms, like lots of little dollhouses."

I watch her carefully. "You must miss Daniel."

She glances away and chuckles dryly. "Oh, yeah."

"Does he like Oxford? I don't think my sister likes university. She seems really different at the moment."

"He likes it," she says quietly. "He's always so busy so…"

We walk in complete silence for a moment.

"I can't wait to grow up," Audrey finally says softly. "I'm going to America. To sing."

I glance at her. "America's so far away."

"Exactly."

"Oh."

"You can come with me! I'm going to New York. There's tons of bookshops there, you'd love it."

"There's a bookshop here in Juniper," I remind her.

"Yeah, but you'll have read all of those by the time we leave," she replies quickly. "Addie, New York would be way better than here! Nobody would think you're weird, they wouldn't treat you so bad."

"I don't know," I say nervously. "Big cities… that's a lot of noise. A lot of sensory stuff."

"Big cities are great for disappearing and then standing out when you want to," she says hungrily. "You could be invisible if you want to be."

I smile at her. She doesn't get it. I am invisible. The real Addie is behind a mask of social rules, regulations and strange neurotypical customs.

"I'll definitely come and visit you," I tell her.

She grins. We continue to walk.

"Here!" she suddenly exclaims.

She grabs my arm and I flinch before I can stop myself. She lets go as if she's been burned. I feel my cheeks flush with embarrassment, red with sorry.

"S-sorry," I mumble, pulling at my sleeve.

I can feel her looking at me, while my eyes are glued to the muddy path beneath my grubby trainers.

"You don't like people touching you," she says quietly.

An observation rather than a question.

"I-I," my hands start to tremble and I feel the sparks in my palms and the electricity in my head. "I'm sorry. I have really strong senses. Sometimes, touch and noise and light can be a bit much. Especially if I'm not expecting it."

"You don't like hugs?"

I feel guilty but I still can't look up. "Only from Keedie. She's the only one."

"Oh."

The trees moving in the wind are the only sound. I eventually settle and am able to look up at Audrey.

"Where are we going?"

She seems relieved to be talking about something else. She jerks her head in the direction we're walking and we run up a small mound and turn the corner.

It's Miriam Jensen's house.

It's a tall, towering old house that looks worn down and forgotten about. Dilapidated, my thesaurus might say. The front garden is large but completely overgrown. The grass is wet and as green as could be. There's an old, crumbling wall and a gate that's hanging off its hinges. A rockery that can't have been touched in months.

The front door of the house is tall and dark and menacing.

"Isn't it spooky?" Audrey whispers, hunkering down behind the wall and staring up at the house.

"Yeah," I agree, kneeling down next to her. "It's Miriam Jensen's house."

Audrey stares at me. "You know the person who lives in there?"

"No," I say softly. "Well, I don't really know her. I just know of her."

"Is she as spooky as this house?" Audrey asks incredulously.

"No. She's... different."

"Different how?"

I can never explain different to them. It's a feeling. "Just different."

Audrey peers up at the front of the house. "Dare me to go to the window?"

"Why?"

She grins at me. "Because it's fun."

She doesn't wait for me to dare her. She slithers over the wall and creeps slowly and carefully to the large window at the right side of the house. The windows are dirty and darkened, it's hard to see in.

"Audrey," I whisper. "I think we should go."

"I just want to look in the window," she whispers back.

"We're trespassing."

She stands up straight to peer into the window and then lets out a little shriek. She comes bounding back to my side of the wall, breathless and wild.

I see why in mere seconds.

The front door opens and Miriam appears, looking grumpily bemused.

"Can I help you miscreants?" she barks at us.

"Sorry," Audrey gushes, still on the verge of giggling. "I just like your spooky house."

Miriam rolls her eyes. "Don't you know it's rude to go creeping around someone's property?"

I suddenly notice that she's carrying something under her arm. Something large and solid. She catches me looking and follows my gaze.

"This is Ernest," she says frankly. "He's a tortoise."

She places him on the ground of the front garden and he stares at us.

"You," Miriam points at me. "You're the one trying to get that memorial made."

"Yes," I admit quietly.

"We're going to raise the money," Audrey says proudly. "My dad's giving us five whole pounds towards it."

"You'll need far more than that," scoffs Miriam. "Even then, they won't say yes."

My nerves and fear are nudged out of the way by

stubbornness and curiosity. I take a step towards her and ask, "Why?"

She looks straight at me and some of the hardness leaves her expression. "Because that's not a past to be proud of. It's not pretty. It's not nice. They like nice things here in Juniper. Being nice is more important to them than being good."

"Being nice and being good are the same thing," Audrey says, her face screwed up in confusion. "Aren't they?"

Miriam stares me down, not Audrey, with slightly raised eyebrows. "What do you say about that?"

I know the truth. "They're not the same thing."

"No," she agrees quietly. "And nice is more important than good here. And a big memorial reminding them all of an evil thing the village did hundreds of years ago isn't nice."

I've never really understood nice. I suppose that's what masking is for. To appear nice.

I swallow. "I'm not giving up."

"You should. It won't happen. You'll just get hurt trying."

I look down at Ernest. He is motionless. Unreadable.

"Everyone always says I can't do things," I hear myself saying. "A doctor said I would never speak. Then that I'd never be able to go to school with normal children. And now everyone is saying I can't do this."

I raise my chin and my voice. "I'm sick and tired of people saying I can't."

"Addie!" Audrey hisses in disbelief. Miriam's face doesn't change. She and I stare at one another in silence for a moment before the fight quietens down in me and my shoulders slump.

"I don't know how to change their minds," I tell her quietly.

"Their minds don't change," Miriam says bluntly. She bends down to pick up Ernest and heads back inside the house. As she reaches to close the door, she gives me one final look. "Believe me, I know."

The door closes with a snick.

I turn and head back to the main path in the woods. Audrey trips after me.

"She was every bit as spooky as that house," she chuckles, moving to walk alongside me. "Hey, Addie, do you reckon she's a witch?"

"What?"

"You know, big scary house in the woods. Long grey hair, black clothes. Maybe she's a witch!"

"She's not a witch," I say softly. "I think she's like me."

Chapter Fourteen

Audrey and I are in the school library.

"Is it a dictionary?"

"No, a thesaurus." I open my little pocket thesaurus and show it to Audrey. I flip to the inside cover. Keedie has written my name in her most beautiful handwriting (which is still a little untidy, but I like it) and has put a large heart around it. It's all colourful and bright and it always makes me smile.

Audrey smiles too.

"What's your favourite word?" I ask her enthusiastically. She grins. "Um…gobbledegook."

I laugh in surprise and try to look it up. "Well done, you found a word that isn't in here."

She laughs too. We look up the longest and most ridiculous words that we can until she gets bored. I'm getting better at reading when people no longer want to do something or talk about a certain topic.

As we leave the library and head to Miss Murphy's room, I spot Jenna. She's waiting by the coats and looking at her shoes. I get ready to ignore her but she catches me by the elbow.

"I'm not going into the toilets to get pushed around by Emily again," I tell her firmly. She rolls her eyes.

"No, it's fine." She glares at Audrey until she leaves. These unspoken conversations that neurotypical people have are exhausting to me.

"Why did you stop being my friend?" I ask her outright before she can say anything.

She won't really look at me and when she answers, it's a mumble. "I just like Emily a lot and she says I can't be friends with both of you."

"So you do what she says?"

"She has lots of cool stuff at her house," she whines. "She lends me things. And we're into the same junk. I don't like sharks or books or the things you like."

"I don't like hair clips or nail polish. But I liked being your friend. So it didn't matter."

She is still looking down. I decide I have nothing more to say so I move into the classroom.

We are allowed some quiet reading time at the end of the day so I take out the book about dolphins. I start to read. They're mammals, like us, and social. My brain doesn't light up by anything in the book. The dolphins look smug in all of their photographs. More importantly, they tend to all look very similar. What I love about sharks is how drastically different they all are. So individual.

I switch to my book about witches. When I read about the women being accused of witchcraft because they practiced herbal remedies, I see their faces clearly in my mind. Their confusion, their anger and their frustration. I can imagine them before cackling accusers, trying to protest their innocence. It sounding pointless even to their own ears. I can smell the herbs, the wet grass. The kindling burning in the fireplace. A time before electricity.

Maggie, staring up at shouting, mocking faces. Knowing that they knew it was all lies. Knowing that there was no point in wasting words. I can hear her shallow, calculating breaths. Trying to convince anyone who would listen, "No, they're wrong. I'm the same as you. I am human like you."

Oh, Maggie. I bet you wished you were a witch. I bet in those moments, as they accused you of supernatural powers, you prayed to be able to cast a spell upon all of them. Wished that their lies were actually the truth.

When my hands are restless and I need to stim, I now imagine that they contain magic. That the twitchy feeling is just fire trying to get out. If I spread my fingers and blast my palm, a shot of magic will fly out. Enough to show all those who belittle and mock that there is a kind of power they will never touch.

I write Maggie's name on my hand. I like the feeling of the marker pen pressing into my palm.

Keedie is waiting at the gates to walk me home from school. I cry out in delight when I see her.

"Audrey, this is my sister," I introduce them excitedly.

Audrey shakes Keedie's hand and takes in her colourful clothes and long hair. "But… I thought you said she was like you?"

Keedie glances between us. "Oh, no, Addie is much nicer than me."

"Keedie's autistic like me," I explain.

"But," Audrey seems very rattled. "She—You don't look autistic."

"I know, we look just like regular people," Keedie says teasingly, causing Audrey to let out a slightly embarrassed laugh.

"Keedie? Keedie Darrow, is that you?"

We all glance over to see one of the mums at the gate staring at Keedie. She comes striding over, smiling with her lips and not her eyes.

"Goodness, how are you these days, Keedie?"

"Fine," says Keedie stiffly. "How are you, Mrs Boyle?"

"Oh, well. Very well. Duncan is too."

"Good."

"My, but you look so much better these days."

Keedie glances around in discomfort. "Have I been ill?"

"Oh, no I meant the… well, you know." She laughs. A strange, hollow laugh. "You seem cured!"

I sigh. Keedie gets told this a lot. Whenever she's masked very well and passed some invisible test, she gets asked if she's been cured.

"There is no cure," I tell this woman. "We don't want a cure."

"Addie, it's all right," Keedie says quickly. "Let's go. Nice to see you again, Mrs Boyle."

Keedie leads us away. I glance back at Mrs Boyle. She is watching us too, no longer smiling her fake smile.

I open my palm and read Maggie's name, now slightly faded on my palm.

*

It's cold and definitely about to rain, yet Audrey and I are standing outside of Dogood Books with our empty buckets and our flyers. Keedie is leaning against the wall of the shop, keeping an eye on us both without interfering in our campaign.

"Money for the new village memorial?" I call confidently, shaking my bucket.

"Here!" Keedie pushes away from her leaning position and digs in her pockets. She drops some coins into both of our buckets. "Let people think you've already got started."

We gleefully shake our buckets, enjoying the jingling sound.

A car slows down and the window descends to reveal Mr Rudge who lives in the street behind our house.

"What's this for then?"

"We're trying to raise money for a new village memorial," I tell him.

"A memorial for what?"

"Centuries ago," Audrey speaks with quiet excitement, "Juniper found a bunch of women guilty of witchcraft and had them executed!"

Mr Rudge draws back in his car seat, looking startled. "Well, that's a wee bit dark."

"It was a dark time, Mr Rudge!" I jiggle my bucket at his rolled down car window. "That's why we need your support!"

"Financial support!" Keedie calls from the wall.

He looks reluctant but finally reaches into his glovebox to find some money. He drops a five pound note into my bucket.

"Thank you," I gasp. "Thank you so much, Mr Rudge."

He smiles nervously and the car pulls away.

"A whole five pounds!" I shout to Keedie, who waves back at me.

"Money looks different up here," Audrey remarks, examining the fiver.

"It's a Scottish fiver!"

"Is it worth more?"

I think for a moment before saying, "Yes!"

"Oh. Well, how much more will we need?"

"Not much more," I say assertively. "A memorial can't cost more than twenty pounds."

"Yeah."

We stand outside the bookshop with our buckets for another hour, and have fourteen pounds and twenty pence before the heavens open and the rain starts to crash down around us.

"Addie, come on," Keedie puts an arm around both of us. "Gotta take Audrey home."

I glance at the shop. "Can I wait in the bookshop?"

Keedie looks hesitant. "Don't leave though, okay? I'll drop Audrey off and come back for you so don't move."

"Ok!"

I wave to Audrey and dash inside the bookshop, shaking my head like a dog to get rid of stray raindrops.

"Don't get the books wet, Addie!" Cleo laughs from behind the desk.

I think she's joking. I try smiling. It works.

"How's the campaign going?" she asks warmly.

"Good. We're almost at fifteen pounds!"

She smiles gently at me and nods.

"I'm waiting for my sister," I gesture to the children's section in the back. "Can I have a look?"

"Absolutely."

I move past the travel books, the grown-up books and the magazines to the small children's section. I love all of the colours. I find a reference book and sit down in one of the beanbags to read.

I'm just turning the page to read when the bell tinkles and the shop door opens.

I glance up to see if it's Keedie but my stomach lurches as I realise it's Emily and what must be her father. I briefly remember seeing him at a parent's evening last year. He was on his phone a lot.

They haven't noticed me.

"What were the books Mum said?" Emily's father addresses Emily. His voice sharp.

Emily looks meek. Different. She takes a small list from her bag and passes it to Cleo, her eyes downcast.

"I can order these in for you, sure," Cleo says kindly. "But... they're a little young for you, my lovely. We have some great books here in the shop."

"She's struggling with reading," Emily's father says bluntly. "She can't keep up with other children her age, she needs younger books."

I hold my breath. Emily looks miserable, unable to meet Cleo's gaze.

"Audiobooks might help with that," Cleo says, ignoring Emily's dad and talking to Emily. "You can listen to them in the car and before bed. Maybe read along at the same time?"

"Just those books on the list, please," Emily's dad says curtly.

"Well, you can have a look in the shop while I put these through the system," says Cleo brightly. "Addie, maybe you can show her some good choices?"

I wince. Emily's eyes shoot up and lock onto me. I expect her to look angry, to sneer, to explode with rage.

Instead she looks scared. Not even scared, petrified.

Before I can say anything, she turns and flees from the shop, the door slamming firmly closed behind her. The bell is shrill and indignant. Her father and Cleo look astonished.

"Have those books here by the end of the week!" he manages to bark as he disappears out of the shop after her.

Cleo and I remain in stunned silence. I gingerly return the book I was reading to its shelf. I edge towards the counter.

"What happened there?" Cleo pushes her pink hair out of her face and starts typing book titles from Emily's list into the ancient computer.

"She's in my class at school."

Cleo eyes me carefully. "But you're not friends?"

"Um," I choose to look at the books instead of Cleo, the eye contact becoming too much. Too invasive. "Not really."

"She's not helping with your witch campaign then?" Cleo asks with a smile.

I don't know if she thinks the idea is silly or not. "No, it's just me and Audrey right now."

"The English girl?"

"Yes."

"Well, I've had some people take your flyers," Cleo says brightly. "And I think it's a grand idea."

The shop bell tinkles and Keedie appears, completely drenched from the downpour. I can tell she is out of energy, defeated by the weather, and ready to go home.

"Not going to be a pleasant walk home, Ads," she says glumly. "Complete dreich out there."

Dreich is sadly one of the many Scottish words that I can't find in my thesaurus. It means bleak and miserable.

As we walk home, Keedie holds her satchel over my head as a makeshift umbrella.

"I was really proud of you at the last village meeting," she finally says.

"You were?"

"Yes. I know all of that masking must have been hard."

Of course she knows.

"I can't seem to get them to listen," I admit faintly. I think about what Miriam said. "I don't know how to make them change their minds, Keeds."

She considers this for a moment as we walk. "Well, what are the facts?"

I think. "That Juniper wrongfully killed lots of women many years ago."

"And why is that important now? Why should people care about that today, it was a long time ago?"

I know she's asking these questions to make me think harder but I don't like it. People should do the right thing because it's a good and proper thing to do. That makes the most sense to me.

"It matters because when a person does something bad, they have to apologise and make amends."

"Well," Keedie shrugs and wrinkles her nose. "Who cares about something that was centuries ago?"

"It doesn't matter the time," I say sternly. "In fact,

that makes it worse. That it's taken so long."

"Everyone involved is dead, why is it important?"

"Because it is!" I snap. "Because it scares me, Keedie. If they don't see it's wrong, if they don't say it's wrong, it can happen again. It could happen to you, it could happen to me. It's already happened to Bonnie!"

"Addie."

"No!" I feel the bad, panicky feeling creeping over me. The heat on the back of my neck, the pulsing in my ears. "Don't tell me it's not the same, it is the same."

"I know it is," she says gently, pulling me into a hug.

I'm shaking a little, not because of the rain.

"Addie," Keedie speaks so softly, just loud enough to be heard over the rain. "People don't want facts. Facts are for roof tiles and weather reports. They want stories. You have to tell them the whole story."

I breathe heavily against her coat and feel water on my face. "Why can't they just care?"

She squeezes me once, quickly. "I know, kid. I know."

I stare up at her. "What's up with you?"

"You know what's up with me, we're the same."

"No." I'm not going to let her joke her way out of this. "Something is not right with you, I can tell."

"Addie, this weather is rubbish, let's get home."

I plant my feet on the heavily soaked pavement and

blink up at her, against the rain. "You always used to tell me everything."

"Adults can't tell children everything, Addie," she says shortly. "Okay? They just can't."

"You're not an adult, you're Keedie."

She laughs, bitterly. "Well, all right."

"What can't you tell me?"

"Addie." For once, she sounds like Nina. "Let's just go, okay?

She walks ahead without me, expecting me to follow. The rain rails down upon her and she looks completely alone.

I run to catch up.

Chapter Fifteen

Keedie seemed exhausted on the walk home. I'm still thinking about it today at school, about the dark circles under her eyes and how she isn't as talkative as usual.

We're allowed into our classroom early because of the rain, so I put my books down by my chair and go to the toilet. I splash my face with water and look at my reflection. I don't often think about how I look but I try to see if I can find any of Keedie in my face. I pull my hair down by my cheeks to make it look longer. I know I don't look like Nina. Although they're twins, they're not identical. Keedie's face is rounder and softer, while Nina is very 'chiselled'. That's how Mum describes her.

I wonder what Maggie looked like. What kind of face did she have? What did any of the so-called witches really look like?

I wash my hands and relish the cold sensation of the water against my warm skin. I shake them dry, enjoying the feeling, and make my way back to the classroom. I feel a little overstimulated but nothing that I cannot regulate. However, as I enter the room, something is not right.

Miss Murphy isn't here yet but almost everyone is gathered in a huddle at the back of the classroom. I look for Audrey and see her by the window, covering her face with her hands. I'm confused. I can't work out what's happening.

"She's here!" someone whispers.

They all part and Emily is revealed, smiling in a frightening way. Malevolent. The word from my thesaurus springs into my mind. She throws something at me. It hits my shoulder and seems to break into pieces. I look down.

It's my thesaurus.

They've taken scissors to it. I sink to my knees, trembling hands brushing against the ripped pages, the spine is broken completely.

"My… my…"

My voice doesn't sound like it belongs to me. It sounds far away.

I open the front of the tiny little book. Someone has taken a dark and ugly black pen and written a word over the drawing Keedie did for me. The sight of it causes something in me to snap. Water splashes against the page and the horrendous word, and I realise that I am crying.

Retard.

"My book," my voice is hoarse.

Someone has violated my little book. Taken the ugly, the cruel and the unfair and carved it into my joy.

I can hardly breathe. I look up at everyone. Jenna is staring at the floor. Emily is hungry for my reaction. Audrey looks mortified and everyone else seems both curious and uncomfortable.

I can read them all. All of them are transparent.

"How could you?" I hear myself rasp.

"I tried to stop her," Audrey murmurs. "But it was too late."

I look up at Emily. "Why?"

She glares down at me, nostrils flaring and eyes aflame. "Because I'm sick of that stupid little book. Sick of all your books."

"WHY?" I scream.

She looks startled for a millisecond. "Because! You're no better than me, retard."

She spits out the word with poison. I look at the rest of the class. Most of them I've gone to school with since I was four.

"You all just stood there!" I yell, my voice strained. "You stood there and did nothing!"

If any of them look ashamed, I can't see it. My vision is blurred. Blood is thumping in my ears.

"You hate her because she's so much smarter than you," Audrey says to Emily, her voice shaking. "You can't stand it."

"She's not," Emily snarls. "She just thinks she is, with her stupid books and her stupid disease. You don't get a free pass just because you have a disease."

I get to my feet, unevenly. My body feels as if it is floating a few inches above the ground. I can vaguely hear Audrey correcting Emily with fury, telling her I don't have a disease. It sounds like an echo. Jenna's silence is louder. All of their silence is loud.

I stare down at the book. At the word.

I feel myself slipping away. I'm not a tree like Keedie said. I'm not anything. All I can see is the poor, broken spine of the book and that word. Audrey is beside me, trying to gather the pieces together.

"Keedie can get you another," Audrey says, her voice sounding like it is underwater. "It'll be okay!"

I don't believe her. But then I hear Emily say something about Keedie. I don't even know what. All I know is I'm flying. I'm flying through the air and I land squarely on top of Emily, as I did on Mrs Craig all of those years ago. I hear shouting, screaming and people rushing around. I'm dimly aware of Emily shrieking beneath me as my fists flail and come raining down upon her. I hear doors slamming and then someone is gripping my arms tightly and hauling me away. Grown-up voices are frantically speaking to one another and I feel my mind shooting, like an electric current.

"Addie!"

It's Mr Allison who has pulled me away from Emily. She is bawling in the corner with one of the playground monitors. They must have heard the screams. Mr Allison's concerned face is in front of mine and he's trying to bring me back into the room.

An Epaulette shark can shut down all of its organs to survive. I feel like that is what is happening to me. My body is in the room, overstimulated and overused, but my mind is gone. It's flying away.

When I return to the scene, Miss Murphy has arrived. She is listening to a tearful Emily.

"She just attacked me," Emily blubbers. "For no reason."

"Liar!" Audrey snaps.

"You be quiet," Miss Murphy snaps back. "If I want to hear from you, I'll ask you."

Mr Allison is crouched beside me and he looks so worried, it makes me ashamed. I am so ashamed. I know not to hit. It felt out of control at the time, I still feel out of control now. But I know it's not right to hit.

"You," Miss Murphy is standing over me, looking more fearsome than I've ever seen her. "Get up."

I stagger to my feet. She grabs my arm and marches me firmly to the quiet part of the classroom and shoves me down.

"You will sit here in isolation until the end of the day. And your parents will be called in."

I don't bother to tell her that Dad is on a closing shift at the supermarket tonight, and Mum is on nights. I can hear Mr Allison quietly protesting, but Miss Murphy says something sharp and asks him to leave.

He does.

I sit with my back to the rest of the class. I can feel people glancing over at me. I don't care. I've been tried and found guilty, there is no way to win now. Miss Murphy will never understand the hurt of that word, I don't even think Emily can possibly understand.

The comments on the online video spring into my mind. Hundreds of strangers saying all of the worst things that you tell yourself, making them feel true. I want to lay down in the corner of the classroom and sleep; my brain feels like it needs to switched off and on again.

But I just wait.

I'm sorry, I'm sorry, I'm sorry, I'm sorry.

Chapter Sixteen

I'm sitting in a small and dark office. Miss Murphy is opposite me. We are waiting for Nina, who was at home when the school receptionist phoned to tell her what had happened and ask could she come in to discuss it? I can hear the clock on the wall ticking, as well as the regular coughs of the school secretary in the next room.

"You are a vile girl."

Miss murphy's voice is quiet and deadly. I look up. She is glaring down at me, no longer trying to hide her face. I see it all. All the colours of her hate.

"Attacking Emily like an animal. I knew you were lazy and badly behaved, but even I could never have..."

"I'm not lazy," I breathe.

"Oh, yes you are. I know you copied on that maths test. I know you cheated."

I'm confused. Then I remember. My workings. My way of doing it. "I didn't copy."

"Don't lie," she snaps. "We'll discuss all this when your sister gets here."

I shut up.

"Part of the problem," she says silkily, "is that your useless parents are never around to discipline you."

I raise my eyes, anger sparking inside of me. "They're working."

"They think slapping a label on you will excuse all of your bad behaviour. Well, guess what, my girl? It won't. It didn't with your sister."

I feel a prickle of rage but I squash it down.

"She gave me hell," Miss Murphy says quietly. "Good as gold with some, a demon with me. And you're no different."

I feel myself flush. I was never trying to be a demon. But doubt floods me. Maybe I was? Maybe I was giving Miss Murphy a really hard time without realising it.

I shake the thought out of my head. I feel like Maggie. Being told over and over that I am one thing, when I know it can't be true. But if Miss Murphy keeps saying it, I might start to really believe it.

"Neither of you should be in this school, it's not right," Miss Murphy adds, sounding almost desperate. "I have thirty-three other children to teach, then you having tantrums over the smallest thing. It's not fair on them. It's not fair on me. I've been teaching for thirty years! Every year, more children than the last. And more problems like you that they're happy to thrust on me with no support."

"It was a meltdown, not a tantrum," I croak.

"Be quiet!"

Her breath is too on my face. I look away, heart pounding and head aching. I know it was wrong to hit Emily. I knew the moment I did it. But I don't think I'm badly behaved. I live my life, desperately trying to make other people feel at ease. To show them I'm normal. That I can be just like everyone else.

And on days like today, when I fail, I hate myself. More than anyone else can hate me.

I silently beg Nina to hurry up. I don't know what to say to Miss Murphy to make it better. I don't know how to tell her that I'm not bad, or at least that I don't mean to be. That I work so hard to be good.

"That poor girl," sighs Miss Murphy. "She'll have bruises for a few days but those scars will last a lifetime."

She means Emily. I want to tell her that I'm sorry, I want to tell Emily that I'm sorry. But I don't think they will believe me. Even if they know it's true.

I can hear voices outside and relief suddenly floods thought me. The door opens and Nina appears. I can tell by her make-up that she was in the middle of filming a video when the school rang. I feel instantly guilty. Then, to my shock, Keedie appears behind her. I hear Miss Murphy sharply inhale.

Nina looks at me, her face all worry. She moves quickly to pull up a chair next to me. "We came as quickly as we could, Miss...?"

"Murphy."

"Miss Murphy."

Miss Murphy taught Keedie but not Nina. They were put in different classes. Miss Murphy is clearly not happy that Keedie is here, even I can read that. She is staring at my sister with the same anger that she has for me. I look up at Keedie, who refuses to sit. Her arms are crossed and she is staring Miss Murphy down. I know how uncomfortable long eye contact can be for Keedie, as it is for me, so I'm amazed to see it.

"Your sister," Miss Murphy pulls her gaze from Keedie to Nina, "is possibly going to be suspended."

Nina glances quickly at me, her expression frantic. "Please... I don't... can I ask why?"

"Certainly," Miss Murphy sits up straight in her swivel chair. "She physically attacked another student. For no reason. Flew at her and beat her viciously. I cannot allow students to feel unsafe in my classroom, suspension is the least I can do to assure Emily's parents that it will not happen again. Exclusion would be my preferred choice, really."

"Addie would never," Keedie speaks quietly but with sharp intensity, "attack someone for no reason. Never, ever."

"She means that Addie has been strictly taught never to hit," Nina hurries to add. "And, she's right, Addie has never hit anyone before. She knows not to." She looks at me. "You know not to."

"I know," I whisper hoarsely. "I'm sorry, Nina."

"It only takes one instance," Miss Murphy continues. "And as I see no real remorse in her manner—"

"What happened, Addie?" Keedie is next to me, eyes wide and kind. "What went wrong?"

"Nothing went wrong, your sister is wrong," snapped Miss Murphy. "I've had difficulties with her since day one. She shouldn't be in my class. She shouldn't be in this school. She clearly needs someone who is used to handling children like her. Violent children. She isn't right for a regular school."

Keedie looks back to my teacher and her face scares me. I have never seen my sister look this way. Full of rage. "I seem to remember you making up things about me too," she tells Miss Murphy, her voice full of black ice.

"Keedie, don't you dare," Nina says. But she also turns to me. "What did happen, Addie? You have to tell us."

"I…" I can see Miss Murphy is breathing heavily and glaring at me. "I was upset."

I want to tell them everything, but the words won't come. They're crumpled on the floor of the classroom. Just as my story was. I can't express how I feel, what I mean to say. It sits at the surface but I can't access it.

"We have a zero-tolerance policy when it comes to bullying in this school," Miss Murphy says sternly.

"Oh, yeah, what if it's the teacher doing the bullying?"

"Keedie!" Nina snaps at her twin, but she doesn't look angry, she looks scared. "Stop."

Keedie ignores her. She stands at her full height, with a slight smile on her face. "You look… nervous, Miss. Almost afraid. What's the matter? Am I too big now?"

I glance back to Miss Murphy. It's true, she looks a little shifty with Keedie close to her. She doesn't seem as confident as before.

"I guess I'm not as easy to bully anymore, am I? Not an easy target now. But lucky for you, you've got my little sister. And she's too young to know that you're a disgraceful, ignorant, ableist coward!"

"Keedie!"

Nina shouts and I am shocked. I can't imagine speaking this way to a teacher. I stare up at Keedie, wondering what has possessed her.

"Let me guess," she goes on, still ignoring Nina. "You've decided that Addie's copied someone else's work, haven't you? Because a little autistic girl could never do something complex all by herself. Only you know good and well that she can, it just kills you. It kills you that you're not able to teach her anything, that everything worth knowing she has taught herself!"

"You are every bit as vile as I remember," says Miss Murphy coarsely, using the same word of Keedie that she used for me. "Still completely disrespectful."

"You're right, I have zero respect for you," Keedie says. "And I know that even if Addie did something wrong today, you're the one that's been doing something wrong since day one. Because I know you, Miss. I remember you vividly. And I know now what I didn't know at eleven. That you have no business being anywhere near children, let alone autistic children."

Miss Murphy is spluttering, looking to Nina for support. Nina doesn't seem to know what to say. Keedie crouches down next to my chair, concern replacing her anger.

"Addie," she says calmly. "What. Happened?"

Before I can answer, there is a knock at the door. Miss Murphy looks hopeful, knowing that someone may be coming to her rescue. "Enter!"

Mr Allison comes into the already crowded room, followed by Audrey. I notice that she is clutching all the remains of my thesaurus.

My heart breaks again to see it.

"Yes, Mr Allison?" Miss Murphy's relief has faded a little.

"I wanted to come and lend my view to the proceedings," Mr Allison says, nodding at my sisters by way of introduction. "I was there for the end of the incident."

"And I saw the whole thing," Audrey says firmly.

"Addie was provoked," Mr Allison tells Nina and Keedie. "Her property was defaced and she was humiliated in front of the class. Not that I'm excusing the behaviour, but I know—well, we all know, it was very out of character."

"Defaced property?" Keedie looks from me to Mr Allison.

Audrey holds out her hands.

"No!" I cry, not wanting Keedie to see it. I don't want her to feel what I felt. "Keedie, don't!"

Keedie takes the remains of the thesaurus from Audrey. Nina moves quickly to stand by her side and see what has happened. They don't know what they are looking at for a moment before Nina gasps, her hands flying to cover her mouth.

"Oh, Addie, your thesaurus."

Keedie's face is unreadable as she brushes her hands over the broken little book and its ripped-out pages. Then she turns over the front cover.

"No," I plead, my voice cracking.

I cannot stop her from seeing it. Nina sees it too. She lets out a low moan as she sees the word written in harsh black pen. Keedie doesn't react.

"It's unacceptable," Mr Allison says quietly. "The culprit should be here to explain themselves."

Keedie turns to face Miss Murphy, holding up the page with the word on it. "You left this part out of your story."

Miss Murphy looks uncomfortable. Not ashamed, but uncomfortable. "Nothing excuses violence."

"But this explains it, you monster," yells Keedie, loudly enough that Nina grabs her elbow and pulls her backwards.

"I will not have violence in my classroom," snaps Miss Murphy.

"This is violence," Keedie waves the page and gestures to the broken book. "This is a different kind of violence. It's obviously caused her to meltdown."

"I'm sorry for hitting Emily," I stammer, scared of all the shouting. "I know I shouldn't have done it.

Something just snapped when I saw my book."

"It's true," Audrey says. "Emily was goading her, saying awful things. In front of everyone." Her voice quivers a little. "It was horrible"

Nina gathers the thesaurus together and shoves it all into her bag. "You let us sit here," she says, her voice sounding more dangerous than I've ever heard it. "You let us sit here and think our sister was the only one in the wrong. I'm so disgusted, I can't even…"

Like me, Nina cannot express herself in this moment. I've never seen her speak to a grown-up like this before.

"You could have got her suspended or worse!" she goes on, her voice loud and angry. "Do you know what happens to autistic children when they slip through the cracks? Because of bigots like you!"

"I suggest," Mr Allison speaks loudly and calmly, "that we schedule another meeting, one that includes Emily Foster, and we resolve this then. Emotions are very high at present… understandably."

"Done," snarls Nina, grabbing my hand and marching me to the door. She stops just before we leave, roughly putting my coat on for me. "And if you think that I won't raise your conduct and treatment of my sister with higher authority, then you are dreaming!"

Chapter Seventeen

The three of us walk home without speaking. Maybe, like me, my sisters have no idea what to say.

"I really am sorry," I finally manage.

Nina looks down at me, slightly dazed. "We know you are, Addie. It was wrong of you but we know you're sorry."

"You did exactly… what I would have done," Keedie says quietly, and that makes me feel a little better. I do notice that she's breathing hard, and she looks completely exhausted. Her words are slow.

"Nevertheless," Nina sighs, "I'm glad you know it was wrong."

"Why didn't you tell us straight away?" Keedie asks. "It's completely understandable, Addie."

"I didn't want to say it to you, Keedie," I say softly, feeling hopeless. "I didn't want it to hurt your feelings, too."

Nina closes her eyes as if she's in pain. Keedie squeezes my hand. "Addie, I heard that and worse when I was in Murphy's class. Don't you worry about me."

But as I look up at her tired eyes, her chapped lips

and her pale face, I cannot help but worry. Something is wrong with Keedie. It has been for a while. I can't name it, I don't know how to help, but I can see it.

"Addie, can we talk just the two of us for a bit?"

Both Keedie and I are surprised by Nina's question.

"Sure, Nina."

Keedie tells us she will see us back at the house, and Nina and I move to an old stone wall to sit. Nina watches Keedie walk away and the worry I feel is reflected in her face. Keedie moves slowly and carefully, as if every step is a colossal effort.

I'm scared for her.

I stare at the ground, worried that Nina's going to tell me off again. But she doesn't. We sit in silence for a while. Letting the Scottish October wind crash and rage around us.

"Addie, I'm sorry," Nina finally says, barely heard over the wind. "I'm so sorry."

"Why?" I ask, completely baffled.

"That woman," Nina shakes her head, "that awful woman. Has she always treated you like this?"

"She hasn't liked me since we met," I admit. "I don't know why. We just don't get on the way I do with Mr Allison."

"It's because she's a bully, Addie," Nina says firmly.

"She's a bully, and girls like that Emily treat you the way they do because Miss Murphy allows it. She does it, so they think they can too."

I suppose that must be true.

"I'm sorry for making you be in that video," she adds. "I'm sorry for everything. I haven't been a very good sister."

"You have, Nina."

"No, I haven't. I... I've always found it difficult, knowing you and Keedie have this bond."

"But Keedie's your twin."

"Yes, but I'm not like the two of you. You have your own language, your own special code. I've always felt a bit left out."

"But that's how the rest of the world makes us feel sometimes," I try to explain. "So we have each other. We have our code because everyone else speaks in ways we don't always understand."

"I know," Nina assures me. "I know. And I'm glad you have each other. It's just... hard sometimes."

She sniffs. "You know, I just don't want you to have the same experience Keedie had."

"What do you mean?"

"I," for once, Nina is the one who cannot make eye contact. "I never appreciated how much she was up against. We were in different classes. I had Mrs Bright, and she just loved every child. Always encouraged us, read to us, gave us presents at the end of each term. And Keedie had... her."

Miss Murphy.

"I had so many friends," Nina laughs bitterly. "And you know, I got to decide who was cool in the group and who wasn't. People followed me around. I felt important. And when they would talk about how they couldn't believe Keedie and I were related, I would agree with them. Encourage them."

I listen, saying nothing.

"Mum made us have a joint fourteenth birthday party," she continues. "Keedie begged her not to, but she was determined. I invited all of my friends. No one but Bonnie came for Keedie."

I vaguely remember it happening.

"They all made fun of the two of them," Nina reveals, her voice scratchy. "And I said nothing. But Keedie let them all have it when they turned on Bonnie. She was fierce! She didn't care what they said to her, but she wouldn't let them touch Bonnie."

It couldn't have been long after that when Bonnie and her mum moved back to England. Northampton. A few months later, she was taken away. I think of Nina sitting at our kitchen table, saying nothing while Keedie confronted her twin's friends. I think of all the children at school who let Emily rip apart my book and write that horrible word.

"And," Nina is crying softly now, staring into the distance with a faraway look. "I never said a word. Never stopped my so-called friends from what they were doing. And where are they all now? They all went to college and university and I haven't heard from a single one. Not one phone call, nothing."

Her shoulders are trembling.

"Keedie has never," she spits the words with pride and pain, "given up on Bonnie. Never. And she never will."

She kicks a stone.

"She was better than all of them. Always was."

I stare up at her, at the sheen in her eyes that tells me she is sad. For once, I know exactly what to say.

"I love you, Nina. I don't need you to be just the same as Keedie. I love you for being you."

She bursts into loud sobs. I jump up, horrified. "I've said the wrong thing!"

"No, it's okay," she's smiling a watery smile. "I'm sorry. I love you, too, Addie. Just as you are. Maybe without the punching."

I laugh.

"Can I hug?" she asks.

"A quick one!"

She complies. A quick but firm hug. I can't remember the last time this happened.

But that doesn't matter, it's happening now.

Chapter Eighteen

I feel happy and relieved as Nina and I walk home. But as we enter the house, I can sense something is wrong. The lights are off, there is nobody downstairs. I look to Nina. She is also frowning, switching the hall light on and calling Keedie's name.

The front door was open, so she must be home. I search the kitchen and laundry room but she's not there.

I run up the stairs, two at a time, and crash into her bedroom.

Empty.

"Oh, Keedie!"

I hear Nina's voice so I hurtle down the landing and into the bathroom. I let out a cry at the sight of Keedie curled up in the corner, looking utterly gone.

Nina is sat beside her, stroking her hair. I edge into the room, terrified and confused all at once. "What's happening?"

"She's experiencing a burnout," Nina says, whispering it so quietly.

"What's that?"

"It's when her system is overloaded and she's so

overwhelmed, she breaks down," Nina explains, still whispering. "She'll be all right in a couple of days. Hopefully."

"Has this happened before?"

"Once, you won't remember," Nina says carefully. "We didn't want to worry you."

For some reason it stings that Nina and Keedie would keep a secret from me.

"Should we move her?"

"No. Just sit here with us for a bit."

I huddle next to them. I can't understand why Nina isn't scared like me. I've never seen Keedie like this, not since that time with Mrs Craig.

"She's been having a tough time at university," Nina murmurs. "Masking very hard. She didn't want to worry you."

"But now I'm worried."

"I know," Nina says and then she chuckles. "What a family we are, eh? What are we like."

Keedie smiles but doesn't speak or open her eyes. Nina is still stroking her hair.

"It's all right, Addie," she says firmly. "She's going to be fine, she just needs a break. This doesn't look anywhere near as bad as the last one. She's just overdone. Don't look so scared."

"Will this… will this happen to me?"

"I don't know," Nina answers honestly. "I don't know, Addie."

When Keedie is able, we move her to her room and help her get into bed. Nina turns the lights off and puts very quiet music on. She then draws me away so Keedie can be alone. But Keedie speaks.

"Addie, stay."

Nina releases me but she doesn't look too pleased. "Keedie, you need to rest."

"It's okay, Nina."

Nina shuts the door and I climb onto the end of the bed.

"I'm sorry, Addie. I don't want you to be scared."

"I didn't know this could happen to you," I blurt out. "I… I don't understand."

"The masking at university has taken a toll on me, I think," she admits. "And I shouldn't have yelled at Miss Murphy."

I wrinkle my nose. "She deserved it."

Keedie smiles. "Yeah, probably. But it was a bit of a breaking point." She nudges me. "We both snapped today."

"Why didn't you say anything? I'm not stupid, I can see how pale and tired you've been."

"Well, you're smarter than me, Addie. I didn't see this one coming."

"Was it like your brain trying to switch off and on again?"

"Yes, exactly like that."

"That's how I felt today?"

Keedie reaches under the bed and hands me a large hardback book. An encyclopaedia on the ocean. I stare at it, dazed. "But…"

"I know you love sharks," she says, "even if you're trying to pretend that you don't. But I thought it might be good to also learn about everything in the ocean. Or at least as much as you can. I was going to give it to you after next week's village hall meeting but I think you need it more now."

I open it and am dazzled by how many pages there are.

"The ocean needs all kinds of fish," Keedie says quietly. "Just like the world needs all kinds of mind. Just one would be really dull, wouldn't it?"

I know what she's trying to say. "I suppose."

"Even on days like today," she says, turning a page for me, a coral reef with so many colourful fish. "Even today, I still wouldn't change you and I wouldn't change me."

"Really?"

"Really. It's not my brain that makes me break down. It's the pretending. The hiding. The way the world isn't built for us."

"You don't have to hide for me, Keedie."

"But you need to understand, Addie," she takes my hand. "I wasn't like you at your age. I wasn't a tree, I was a leaf. I was angry and scared and no one could tell me why I was the way I was. And then, when you were born, I realised we were the same. Or at least similar. And that was great."

She pauses.

"But the more you came to look up to me, the harder it was to talk about the bad days. The difficult days."

"I'm sorry."

"Not sorry, nothing to be sorry for." She exhales. "I was just so afraid of scaring you. Or letting you down."

I try to understand. Keedie always seemed perfect to me. Always knew what to say, what to do, was always able to answer questions. I didn't know that it had come at a price.

"I'm not a tree, Addie," she laughs bitterly. "The wind will blow me away one day."

"No," I say stiffly. "I won't let it."

"Now, you listen to me," she says, closing the book

and moving it to the side. "I want you, at that village hall meeting next week, to tell them your story. Tell them everything. Make them understand why it's so important to you that these people are remembered." She sniffs and wipes at her tired eyes. "Can you do that for me?"

"Tell all those people?"

"You can write down what you want to say," she says eagerly. "But I think that it will make them listen."

"Keedie, I don't know."

"I know it's scary," she says gently. "But take it from me. It's better to be open about who you really are, what you're really like, and be disliked by a few than it is to hide who you are and be tolerated by many."

"Is that why this happened?" I ask.

"I think so. So don't be like me, Addie."

"All I've ever wanted is to be like you."

"Not this time. Be like you. Tell them why it's important. Make them understand. Because, you know what? All I've done this term at university is mask. I've masked so well, I've fooled myself. And the more I've pretended to be like them, the more they've applauded. And the more I've pretended, the more I've felt myself slipping away."

She squeezes me and speaks with a wobble in her voice, "And it's not worth it, Addie. No one is worth feeling that way for. You've got to find the people that accept the real you."

"Like Audrey?"

"Yes. Like Audrey."

I know she's right. It's been so much easier with Audrey than it ever was with Jenna. Jenna would always be so disappointed or disgusted when I was relaxed and myself; I was constantly masking, adapting and hiding.

And I don't want to hide anymore.

"You're my best friend," I say quietly.

She presses her cheek against the top of my head, quick and firm. "And you're my best friend."

She says nothing more about it. We fall asleep side by side.

Chapter Nineteen

I'm sitting in a field writing my speech. Keedie said not to rely on memory, so I'm working it out before the final meeting. One cow is watching me, hair covering its eyes while it slowly chews some cud.

"I don't think this speech is going to change anyone's mind," I tell the cow resignedly.

The cow's nostrils flair.

"My sister hasn't been well," I tell him.

Two more cows are drifting over to see what's going on. Cows are naturally very nosy. They can't help themselves, they're extremely curious and far too trusting.

But very good confidants.

"She was ill and trying to hide it from me," I explain. "I knew something was wrong. I could just tell. But grown-ups are never honest with me."

Three more cows amble over.

"Lots of people aren't honest," I add, scribbling out a word and writing in another. "People say they're fine when they're not. That they're pleased to see you when they're not."

One cow tentatively licks my temple.

"Addie?"

I look up. Jenna is standing by the fence. She's walking her family dog, Pebble. She looks slightly stunned to see me sitting on the grass, surrounded by a herd of inquisitive cows.

I watch her steadily. She makes her way over, her welly boots pink and expensive.

"How…" she fidgets and nervously tugs on Pebble's lead, "how are you?"

I look back down to my notepad and continue to write.

"What are you writing?"

"A speech."

"What for?"

"I'm still campaigning for my memorial."

"Oh," Jenna peers at what I'm writing. "For those witches?"

"Yes."

"You haven't given up."

"No."

"Addie," her voice is coloured with desperation. A sickly, white colour. "I feel bad about what happened."

"So do I," I murmur, starting a new paragraph.

"I know." She moves a little closer. "It wasn't very nice."

I sigh and glance up at her, squinting against the cold October sun. "I don't care about nice, Jenna. I really don't. And I don't care what any of you think of me anymore."

"I didn't know she was going to write that, I swear," she babbles. "Promise. She said she was going to write something but I didn't know it would be that."

"I don't care, Jenna."

I get to me feet and put my notepad under my arm.

"If someone tried to take something that meant something to you, I would've stopped them. If they had called you a name, I would have told them to shut up. That's what friends do. That's what good people do. You just stood there."

"No one knew what to do," she argues, flushing crimson.

"Audrey did. Mr Allison did."

"Audrey," Jenna rolls her eyes and lets out a puff of frustration at the mention of my friend's name. "She's weird, Addie. She doesn't look like us, she doesn't sound like us."

"I don't need my friends to look like me," I say sharply. "I don't need them to sound like me. I don't need them to like everything I like. I don't even need them to think like me. But I do need them to stand up for me when someone writes a horrible word on my present from my sister."

I walk past her and jump over the fence. I don't look back.

*

Keedie seems better. At last.

Mum, Dad, Keedie, Nina and I are walking in the Juniper woods. Walking to see the tree that has haunted me for weeks.

Mum and Dad were not happy about what happened with Emily. A meeting was scheduled but Emily's parents called it off when she finally admitted to them what she wrote in my thesaurus, and how she tore it up. Mum and Dad filed a complaint about Miss Murphy. Audrey and I are spending more and more lunchtimes in the library as the weather worsens, and I asked Mr Allison for help in finishing my speech for the village hall meeting.

Now, we all walk together. Taking in the last days of autumn in Juniper before the village meeting.

"It's important that this doesn't happen again," Mum says firmly.

I nod. "I know. I shouldn't have hit her, I know that."

"That's not actually what I mean," Mum says. "I know you're sorry. I know you know that's not how to behave, but what she did was awful."

"It was," Dad and Keedie both say in chorus.

"She did that intentionally to cause harm," Mum goes on. "If you'd done something like that to another child, I'd be very worried."

It's true, it had never occurred to me to tear up someone else's things and write evil words on the broken pages.

"I saw something I wasn't supposed to see," I say, and the all turn to look at me.

"What?" Mum looks worried.

"When I was in Dogood's, looking at the books, Emily and her Dad came in," I stare at my feet while I tell the story. "Her dad was quite nasty and told Cleo to order some baby books to help Emily with her reading. He said she wasn't keeping up."

Mum lets out a big sigh and shakes her head.

"Well, that explains it a little," Dad says gently.

"She's targeting you because you're such a good reader," Nina explains. "That's what bullies do. They try to make you feel bad about the good things you have. The things that they want."

It doesn't make a great deal of sense to me. Nothing about bullies makes sense to me.

"Addie," Mum sounds firm but not angry. "Has Emily said things to you, done things to you, before this event with the thesaurus?"

"Um," my brain conjures up memories, plays them like montage. "She's called me stupid a couple of times. And said no one wants to eat lunch with me. And that I would have been burned as a witch hundreds of years ago."

Mum stops in her tracks and makes a strange noise. Dad quickly squeezes her shoulder and they have one of their silent communications, one that I can't read.

Keedie tosses her hair and looks to me, colour starting to return to her face. "Addie, what did all of those villagers here in Juniper do when their neighbours were being dragged away on false charges?"

It seems like a trick question. "What did they do?"

"Yeah, what did they do?"

"Well… nothing."

"Exactly!

I think of the shame and pain Nina had felt about letting her friends bully Bonnie and Keedie while she had said nothing. I think of how the witches must have felt, as they were dragged through these woods, to look out and see the faces they had perhaps known their whole lives.

"All those kids in your class stood by and did nothing," Keedie continues.

"Not Audrey," I whisper.

"I think," Keedie kicks some pebbles out of her path, "I'd rather be burned for being a witch than stand by and watch it happen."

"No one is burning anyone," Mum says curtly. She turns to me. "Addie, if Emily has been doing this all term, it's important that you tell an adult."

"She couldn't exactly tell that teacher," Dad points out.

"Then you tell us," Mum smiles sadly at me. "You always tell us. Or Mr Allison. Or one of your other teachers."

I nod, understanding. "I just... I just didn't know grown-ups can be bullies."

Nobody speaks. And the tree stands just ahead of us. I walk towards it, trancelike, and I'm glad that no one is following me. It towers over me with a defiant agelessness. Branches gnarled and threatening, some thin enough to snap in two.

Others that are thick enough to throw a rope over.

I touch its bark. Dad said once that you can tell the story of a tree by cutting it open. I sometimes feel that way. I can't always express what I'm feeling out loud.

But with paper and pen, I can make sense of everything.

There would be no paper without trees, even cursed ones like this.

I think of when Miss Murphy tore up my writing. I know she couldn't have fully understood what she was really doing. Taking my voice away.

When it happened, I was afraid. Embarrassed. I had told myself off, looked down at the words she was saying looked repulsive and disgraceful. I had told myself that even though I could not understand why she was angry, that she must have been right. As she scolded me, I absorbed the words. Allowed them to sit inside my skin.

But she was wrong. She was wrong to do it.

I spend every moment of my life, when I am outside of our family home, second guessing everything that I think and do. I study people's faces to make sure that they are accepting what I am saying, that they are never confused or offended.

I make myself smaller. I shrink away, eyes downcast and hand outstretched. For a crumb of sympathy.

Are any of them ever doing the same for me? Do they ever think how hard it can sometimes be, to hear everything and feel everything so deeply that it can knock you out? Miss Murphy cared more about how my writing looked than the importance of what was written.

She didn't like that I worked in my own way, but didn't care about the answers being correct.

My different way of working, of being, was what infuriated her. My different way of being. And I allowed all of that to affect me. To make me put my shark books away.

Standing in front of this tree, knowing its history, I press my whole palm firmly against its bark. I push until it almost hurts. I imagine that I am pushing all of the horrible words, all of the nasty tones, the eye rolls, the shouting, the demands, the commands, the cruel laughter, the words they want me to hear, the things they think I can't understand, the slow up and down looks, the jibes, the disrespect, the scraps of tolerance and the constant unwillingness to understand.

I push it all into the tree, using both hands. As I do, I feel the shame, the fear, the anxiety of it all transfer into the bark.

I push the horrible word Emily used into it with one final shove.

And I feel free. Because I know, after all of it, that there's nothing wrong with me.

There is nothing wrong with me.

I will not let people use my difference, as a stick to

beat me with. I imagine throwing that stick into the river. Watching it disappear and float away.

I press my forehead against the trunk of this giant tree.

"Mary," I breathe. "Jean." Another breath. "Maggie."

I leap back from the tree, as if I've been shocked by a spark. I breathe heavily, staring up at it. It seems less frightening. Less powerful.

I'm still breathing in and out as Mum, Dad, Nina and Keedie move to stand behind me. No one says anything.

We stand, the five of us, by the tree and the river while all of the past blows away.

And we stand steady.

Chapter Twenty

As I wait for the Juniper village meeting to be called to order, I feel more nervous than ever. It matters more now than it ever did. After everything. Maggie's name is freshly written on my palm. I rock back and forth in my seat while the room bustles around me. I ignore the painful, flickering light on the corner of the ceiling.

"Now," Mr Macintosh looks somewhat wary as he stands at his podium. "Miss Darrow would like to make a speech on behalf of her now infamous campaign. For the small few of you who are not aware, Adeline has been canvassing for a memorial plaque or sculpture to be erected in memory of the Juniper victims of the witch trials. Which happened," he fixed me with a look, "a very long time ago."

Poor Mr Macintosh. Forever worrying about Juniper's reputation. I take the stand and look out at a sea of bemused and expectant faces. My entire family is here, plus Audrey and her parents. Mr Allison too. They all take up the third row and are looking up at me encouragingly.

I take a deep breath and lock eyes with Keedie. She is beaming at me. So is Nina.

"My name is Addie. I am eleven years old and I am autistic."

There's a slight murmur. I go on.

"I am not afraid of this. Or ashamed. It's just a part of who I am. Someone being autistic is no different to being left-handed or colour-blind. It means we experience the world differently. And while some people might misunderstand it, I know that it is just part of who I am. I can't be cured. I don't want to be. It's just a fact of my life."

I take a breath and make sure not to look at anyone. I'm so aware of their attention.

"However, centuries ago, people like me would have faced enormous difficulties. People would have understood even less back then than they do today. Being different was dangerous."

I look briefly at Mr Macintosh and take another breath.

"Centuries ago, someone like me could have been accused of being a witch. Just for being different. I sometimes don't know how to read people or work out how they are feeling. This can lead to misunderstandings. Sometimes my face doesn't show how happy I really am. I might not seem that approachable. And I'm very easy to bully. Sometimes I even start to believe what the bullies are saying."

I look at my hand. At Maggie's name.

"My sister Keedie is autistic, too. And she made friends with another autistic girl at her appointments. Her name was Bonnie. But, after Bonnie moved away, she couldn't cope anymore. With school, with her anxiety. So she got put away. By people who didn't understand her needs. No matter how much she tells them she needs to leave, they won't let her. They don't trust her, they don't think she knows herself."

I sniff, feeling troubled as I remember Bonnie. The bright, laughing girl who had bad meltdowns but was never bad.

"If someone told me that I was a witch for long enough, I might have started to believe them. It seems easier sometimes, doesn't it? To believe the bad things instead of the good."

I lose my place for a moment and look out at the faces. I don't know if it's me, but they seem to be really listening.

"When I heard what was done to these women, right here in Juniper, it hurt my heart. That they were killed merely for being different or weird, and everyone just let it happen and forgot."

I see Mr Macintosh look down at his feet out of the corner of my eye.

"I don't want to forget them. I want us to have a plaque, something small, dedicated to their memory. Our apology."

This was supposed to be the end of the speech but I decide to say one last thing.

"I think different is good. As long as you're not hurting anyone. We need all kinds of difference in the world. And I know some people think that I've been put up to this. All I can say is, if you believe that, you probably don't know any autistic girls."

People laugh.

"I'll finish now," I conclude, "but… I think it would be nice if everyone promised themselves something. And I will as well! When we meet someone and instantly think they're strange or different, we should try to maybe be kind. I may be strange to some of you, but I'm very normal to my family."

Keedie, Nina and my parents laugh out loud.

"And you might seem strange to someone else. But… while you are neurotypical and I'm autistic, I promise. We are more alike than we are different."

I see Mr Macintosh look at his watch.

"My Grandpa always said, people like me in the past might not have been the most sociable. Or the chattiest. But while everyone else was around the fireplace gossiping, we were out finding electricity. That's what my autism is. It's a kind of spark. It's like sharks, you see," I can see my parents glancing at one another, maybe wondering if I'm about to turn this meeting into a three-hour lecture on sharks.

"Sharks can sense the electricity of life itself. It's their superpower. But someone made a horror film about them, and now millions of them are killed each year. Like the witches, for no reason."

I give Mr Macintosh a look to tell him that I'm almost finished. "My autism isn't always my superpower. Sometimes it's difficult. But on the days when I'm finding electricity in things, seeing the details that others might not, I like it a lot."

I realise I've reached an end. And I feel good, no matter what is decided.

"I like myself the way I am. A lot."

I move to sit down. There is a smattering of clapping which leads to quite loud applause, enough that I need to cover my ears. Keedie and Nina quickly hug me.

An assembly member whispers something in Mr Macintosh's ear and he nods, moving to the podium.

"We will now deliberate and then vote."

Keedie and I wait outside of the village hall while the committee considers my request.

"Was it okay?" I finally ask.

She pretends to consider my question and then grins. "It was amazing. I'm really proud of you."

I suddenly feel happy and like crying at the same time. "You're not mad I mentioned Bonnie?"

I see a flash of pain. "No. People need to understand." She blows out a breath and it looks like smoke in the air. "You know, I think a lot of people think autistic adults don't exist. Like it's something we grow out of. So no, I'm glad you mentioned Bonnie. They need to know we're still here."

We stand together and watch Juniper in silence for a moment.

"I'm taking a week off from university to go down to England and visit Bonnie," Keedie eventually says.

"Can I come?"

She laughs and presses her hand to my face. "Of course not, Addie."

"But I want to tell her what I did today!"

"I'll tell her for you, okay?"

I open my mouth to argue but then notice Audrey approaching us. She is waving excitedly.

"That was awesome!" she gushes, grabbing my hands and jumping up and down.

I laugh, giddy at her appreciation. "Thanks."

"I'll see you inside," Keedie tells me, smiling at Audrey and heading back into the hall.

"So I got you something," Audrey says, digging in her large anorak pocket.

I wait in surprise, not knowing what to say.

She pulls out a little book and hands it to me with a flourish.

I look down and read the title: Scots Thesaurus.

"It's a pocket thesaurus," she says gleefully, "with Scottish words included."

"What?" I cry out in delight. "Audrey, that's… I don't…"

"It's okay," she says gently. "You deserve it. And I'm sorry it's not your old one."

"No, this is…" I stroke the little book. "This is just as good. Thank you."

She takes a deep breath and adds, "I'm so sorry for what she did. What they all did."

"Yeah, well," I shrug, still marvelling over the thesaurus. "I don't care what they think of me."

"And do you know," she laughs nervously. "I actually thought about it. I think dolphins are actually really boring."

I feel myself grinning. "Really?"

"Yeah. I've been reading more about sharks." She smiles at me, a secret smile. "I think they're much better."

I suddenly hug her. And I don't mind it. It isn't too tight or too controlling. She hugs me back.

Because we're friends. Best friends.

Chapter Twenty-One

The plaque for the witches is unveiled near the end of October.

The whole village seems to be here to see it, including a newspaper which makes Mr Macintosh very happy. He makes a speech telling the journalists that he has always supported the idea and was thrilled upon reading that other communities in Edinburgh had undertaken similar ventures.

"Now, we have one person to thank in particular for this plaque being completed so quickly," he proclaims proudly to the crowd.

I raise my eyebrows, wondering if he is going to thank me in front of these newspaper people.

"Mrs Miriam Jensen kindly paid for its completion in full."

I gasp in surprise and glance across the crowd. Sure enough, standing apart from everyone is Miriam, leaning on her wooden walking stick and looking on with a grumpy expression. She turns to leave at the mention of her name. I wonder if I can push through all of these people to thank her.

But she seems to vanish.

I step back and exhale. I'll thank her one day.

"So now, without further ado, Juniper presents…"

Mr Macintosh reveals the memorial with aplomb.

"An important part of Juniper's vast legacy!" he says as it is revealed and people applaud.

People clap. I lean in to read what it says.

In memory of the many women wrongly accused and executed for being witches in Juniper. May this plaque honour their lives and promise an end to intolerance.

I nod, satisfied. I don't mind if I don't get any credit. Autistic people have probably done so much for hundreds of years without any credit. Maybe it's a rite of passage.

I say a quiet goodbye to Maggie. To Mary. To Jean. I think of them often, but not as much. Seeing the plaque proudly featured in the village green, with flowers growing all around it, has soothed all of the sadness I felt about their lives. About all of the witches' lives.

I'm proud of Juniper. I've always liked living here. I've always liked that everyone knows who you are, who your family are. I like that people care about making the village a pleasant place to live.

Now Juniper is good. Not just nice.

People clap and photographs are taken. I wave goodbye to my family and run off to meet Audrey at the end of the road. We are going her house to bake shortbread and make our Halloween costumes. We're also planning a trip to London, so Audrey can visit her grandparents and I can see the aquarium.

For Halloween, we've already planned our route for the night: which houses to avoid and which ones give the best treats.

We're going to dress as witches.

Acknowledgments

No one is self-made.

I have to begin by thanking Dr Melanie Ramdarshan Bold and Dr Samantha Raynor for getting me through UCL. It was a thrilling but unfamiliar environment for me and you guided me through some challenging times, when the imposter syndrome was louder and more convincing than ever. Thank you for encouraging me to write about my neurodiversity. And thank you for teaching a class about a certain inclusive publisher.

To Chloe and Robyn for making me laugh when I'm on the edge and when it's super inappropriate.

To Anita, for reading a bartender's short stories when everyone else clicked their fingers and made fun of her.

Thank you to Lauren, agent extraordinaire. Thank you for gently but firmly keeping me calm over phone and email. And thank you for that first meeting in Brixton when you proved how much you cared about your authors.

Thank you to the Big Yin, for reasons both personal and obvious.

Thank you to Anna for the brilliant editorial notes and for getting straight to the point. I had lost all objectivity and you pointed to the cracks.

To my cousin, Aileen, and my extended family. I know I'm the weird one but thank you for never bringing it up.

To Aimée, David and the Knights Of and Round Table Books team. Thank you for taking a meeting with a nobody. Thank you for asking if I had a book in me. I have many, and you were the first to ask. Thank you for everything you're doing and everything you've done.

Thank you to Marssaié and Kay for creating the most incredible cover. I had no clue what this book actually looked like and then you showed me. You knew exactly what to do. You pulled together something that I would fight people in the bookshop for. Thank you!

Eishar. My editor. The editor. I think you saved my life when you gave Addie a seat at the table. Thank you for everything, you're the best of the industry.

To Maddie, my dearest friend. A copy of this book will find its way to Australia, even if I have to carry it over myself. I love you and miss you.

To Book Twitter and everyone who has supported this novel. Bloggers, librarians, booksellers. Change is slow but the changers are incredible.

To Mum. The hardest working person I know. Every time I hit the ground, I can feel you leaning over me to tell me I have twenty seconds to be upset and then I have to get back up and keep going. Thank you for bringing books into the house. Thank you for all of the many sacrifices that I don't deserve. Thank you for the work ethic and the drive.

To Dad. My best friend.
To Josh. There are no words.

And to my two grandfathers, Granny and Mor Mor, I hope you would have been proud of this.

Elle McNicoll
Author

Elle McNicoll is a debut children's author from
Scotland, now living in East London. As a
neurodivergent writer, she is passionate about disability
rights and representation and assists as a mentor for
neurodivergent students at UCL. When she isn't writing
fiction, she works as an editor and in her spare time,
makes colourful chokers for friends to wear. *A Kind of
Spark* is her first novel.

Kay Wilson
Illustrator

Kay Wilson is a London based illustrator with ADHD who creates art inspired by the printing process, British mythology and the work of Tove Jansson. When she's not drawing, she can usually be found hanging out with a cat.

KNIGHTS OF